Cruel N(

Oliver Woodman

First published in 2017 by Endeavour Press Ltd.

Table of Contents

1. Waiting — 1646

Phoebe was disappointed.

She had waited for the return of Praisegod Norton, and he had not come. He had gone away in June 1645 and she had then been confident that he would, as he had promised, return. But he had not.

That summer had faded into winter, and then the spring of the new year had brought fresh life and hope. But now it was nearly twelve months since she had seen him. She began to give up the thought that her life would be altered by him — perhaps she had merely imagined that he had ever wished for marriage. Perhaps she had seen and heard only what she herself wished to see and hear. Had he really said he would take her away from Heathcote House? For that was where she now remained, as the cook to a household that, apart from her fellow servants, had come to consist only of one lonely and disappointed Cavalier.

He, George Chennery, had returned from the war a sad and silent man, his energies lost in the thankless task, now apparently abandoned, of trying to overcome the domestic enemies of King Charles. George had come back to his patrimony only after the Monarch's final defeat, to a house that awaited him in silent expectation. George desperately missed both his recently dead father and his sister, murdered, a casualty of the late civil war. He spent hours walking in solitude across the land that was now his. Of Phoebe's heartache he had no notion. He maintained an icy reserve in all dealings with his servants, and thought, in his inexperience, that this was proper. He did not understand that their devotion to his dead relatives could have been a key to overcoming the sadness that gripped him.

George had finished fighting his war in February 1646, at Torrington, where Parliament's new modelled army, under Tom Fairfax, had beaten the last Royalist force still in the field. George was there when Lord Hopton, its commander, surrendered the following month. Like all of the beaten Royal Officers, he was sent home like a naughty boy by the Parliament men. Before they released him, the victors required a solemn oath binding him in honour not again to take up arms. Most of the

Officers in his position took the oath; those who baulked at it were offered the alternative of indefinite imprisonment.

George gave his oath lightly. He regarded it as having been obtained under duress — as indeed it was — and therefore inviting repudiation. Besides, the words invoked God, to whom George gave little thought, and his honour, which he had never in his heart pledged to King Charles, but rather had subordinated to a love of himself. Even the sacrifice of three years of his life to be a Royalist soldier was something George Chennery had granted to his monarch not from devotion, but mainly because of the social consequences he thought would follow from *not* doing so.

Those social consequences had proved illusory. He found, upon his return home, that many of the neighbouring Northamptonshire landed interest that was his peer group had either managed a surprising neutrality throughout the recent quarrel, or had numbered themselves amongst the King's opponents. Those families that had stoutly embraced the royal cause were now quiet, overwhelmed at the scale of its defeat, and often grieving the loss of husbands and sons. Those dead men were precisely those friends who had so gaily ridden off with George in the summer of 1642, and their absence compounded his isolation, and multiplied his depression.

Phoebe felt no inclination to confide in her master, or to seek his advice. Even if George had been a more approachable man, she knew too much about him. She had grown to be adult alongside him and his sister, and knew that her beloved mistress, the dead Lady Jane, had despised her brother as a fool. Phoebe had come to share that judgement. Thanks to George, every man on the staff of the house, and many of those working on the estate, had gone away with him to join the lost armies of King Charles. They were now, almost to a man, missing. Their women waited, without news of them, and with diminishing hope. It was not as if any of them had been personally committed to keeping the King safe. What was Charles Stuart to *them*?

It was Henrietta, the maid who was herself grieving her absent husband, who Phoebe allowed to see her own misery. One evening as they sat together in the evening sunshine, looking out over the yard of the house, Henrietta said, "Phoebe, how do we find out. whether they are still alive… your Praisegod, my man Henry? It don't seem right. Us being left with no news. Am I a widow? I do not know."

Phoebe had said, "You are right. Maybe Praisegod is dead. He went away just before that great fight at — where was it? — Naseby. How can we find out?"

She thought about all that she knew, all that Praisegod had said about himself and his role in the Parliamentary forces. An idea took shape. She sought the assistance of the Chennery Estate Steward, Jacob, for she could not herself read or write. Jacob was sympathetic, and gave her help — and so a letter was written. Jacob sent it off to Oliver Cromwell.

*

Old John Souter, farming his own demesne in Suffolk, was also finding that a great sadness had engulfed his own returned son.

Josiah Souter had come back to his home in that same summer of 1645, having prematurely resigned his commission as a captain in Parliament's army. John had realised quickly that his son, while showing no wound, was nonetheless damaged by his military experience. However, he imagined that if Josiah were left to himself, with rest and good food and surrounded by the familiar life of the farm and house, his son would heal. Spring, however, gave way to summer, and that same twelve-month period that Phoebe had waited passed also for John — without him seeing the expected rejuvenation of Josiah. The father was grieved, and puzzled as to what more he could do to help.

The passing seasons guided the management of their farm, and the older man found no reason to complain of his son's ready acceptance of his work and responsibilities. Josiah played his part in the hedging and ditching, the ploughing and the sowing. He sat alongside his father as the duties of a magistrate were discharged, and when, as their Squire, John instructed or cajoled his tenants in their troubles. But he had few words for anyone, and while always courteous, took few initiatives to begin conversations.

As ever, John and his son ate dinner together, and every evening after eating they called their dogs to heel and strolled out across their beautiful land. This had been their habit for as long as Josiah could remember, although interrupted by the three years he had been away. Josiah fell again into the routine, but through habit, without the joy they both remembered, without that spark that told his father he was really home.

Josiah did not speak to his father about the experience of being an Ironside Captain. John Souter had never known warfare, and felt himself inadequate. Because of this, he chose not to probe, to uncover the effect upon the self of dealing in death. There was no doubt in either of their minds that the fighting had been necessary, but there was a flatness, an absence of any sense of success or achievement, in the victory.

They read their Bible together as they always had, and prayed. John's prayer — voiced aloud — was always for the welfare of his son, and his grief was magnified when, at that, he sometimes saw tears appear in Josiah's eyes.

One evening, as they sat at dinner, John said, "By the lord Harry, but there are so many bones left in this coney stew! Our Charlotte is getting too ancient to continue as our cook. She can no longer see what she is doing. But then... well, she has been cooking for us since — oh! Since before your mother died. We shall just have to put up with it!"

Josiah suddenly spoke.

"Rabbit Stew. Praisegod made wonderful rabbit stew."

"Praisegod?"

"Oh aye. Praisegod. A good man. Could shoot rabbits. Never missed. And he made a wondrous stew." And Josiah told his father the history of Praisegod, his comrade and his friend.

Josiah's final duty for Parliament's army had been to deliver vengeance upon the murderer of Corporal-of-Horse Praisegod Norton. That sharp action had seen the last of several deaths from the hand of the Ironside captain, Josiah Souter.

Having now begun, Josiah could not stop talking. He told his father of the effect upon himself of seeing the dead at Gainsborough. He told him of the riding down of the King's infantry at Winceby. He told him of the farm in Lincolnshire and the starvation of the winter of 1643. He told him of the strength he had felt at Marston Moor. And of the slaughter there. Above all, he communicated to his father how he had hated his role, how strange it had felt to be there, surrounded by hatred and fighting to the death. How he had made himself do it. He left until last his bitter hatred of the man who he blamed for all the wreckage of the lost lives.

"That man of blood, King Charles, what remorse, what repentance has he shown? The worst of it is this. Despite all those dead men, he is still the King."

His father let him talk himself out, moving gently to keep the wine glass filled. Josiah found himself drinking unusually deeply. As that evening passed, he became fatigued, but memories kept filling his head and new recollections had to be described. It was very late when finally he fell silent, and lapsed into a half unconscious silence. His father summoned help, and Josiah was half carried to his bed.

Old John, too, was exhausted, but felt mightily relieved, convinced that a floodgate had been opened and a mental torment relieved. "Praise the Lord! Praise the Lord!" said John Souter, "Praise Him, for now my son will return to me."

Which proved to be the case. Josiah slept throughout the next day. His father gave instructions that he was not to be disturbed. Later, sitting down alone to his dinner, John was joined by an apologetic Josiah. But the old man was in no way perturbed, because he could see from Josiah's face that at last he had, in truth, a son who had arrived safely home.

*

Some days later, after their evening walk, John found Josiah cleaning a set of pistols. A canvas bag lay to one side.

John picked one pistol up. It was a piece of fine quality. He saw that there was dried blood upon the butt. He looked at his son, raising one eyebrow in enquiry.

"These were Praisegod's. I should have done this months ago. He would want it. We recovered these when we... dealt with his killer. They are wonderful guns, powerful, accurate... and feel how finely balanced they are." Josiah smiled. "We buried three men that day. They were all renegades. The rubbish of war." Then he paused. "There was a woman there, too. What became of her, I wonder... "

John said, "I came to find you because this has come." He laid a letter before his son.

For a moment Josiah looked, without speaking, at the packet. He could see from the seal that it came from the Parliamentary army. He was not, he realised, very interested in its content but duty compelled him to open it.

There were two papers within. Josiah quickly scanned the first and passed it to his father without comment. The older man read merely that it was the second paper that was referred to Josiah, 'for appropriate action'. And a signature. It was 'O Cromwell'.

Josiah's face had lit up as he read the second sheet. "Of course," he said, "from Phoebe." Then he passed the letter to John. It was marked with a cross, and the words, *Phoebe Hetherington, her mark.*

Josiah said, "Phoebe was Praisegod's intended wife, father. She's a cook."

'A cook!' John Souter thought, but he said nothing.

*

Josiah, shortly after that letter arrived, visited Heathcote House to find her and sadly told Phoebe of Praisegod's fate. She wept, as he had known she would.

Before his son left Monks Soham on that errand, John had steeled himself to tell their old cook Charlotte that she must cease her responsibilities and work. He was mightily relieved when she embraced the news with relief. "Ah Master," she said, "Praise the Lord! I would have had to tell you soon — 'tis my eyes you see, I don't see so well now." The Souters could be relied upon to care for a member of their household who had served them well, and Charlotte could rest under their roof until death took her. Her ready acceptance of her changed position made John cheerful again. The conversation, far from being difficult, had been painless. "Praise be!" he muttered, "Thank the Lord!"

Charlotte's acquiescence enabled Josiah to make an offer to Phoebe.

"My house is less grand. We are a working farm, not a great house, Phoebe. My father is a landowner and magistrate, but we have no claim to aristocracy. We need a cook. No, we need more than that. The house needs managing. A housekeeper. You'd be the mother of it, really. But mostly we need a cook. From the praise given to your skill by my friend Corporal Norton, I know that is something you can do. Come to Monks Soham."

Phoebe hesitated. She saw in Josiah's offer much that was unknown. However, she perceived also the enduring chill of Heathcote House. She was persuaded by the warmth of Josiah's tributes to Praisegod.

And so, Phoebe came to Monks Soham.

*

While the Souter household gained a feminine house manager — a role which Phoebe came to exercise wonderfully well — there was a departure too.

Josiah was concluding his direction of the ditching and hedging of ten-acre field, which was the piece of ground farthest from his house that they owned. The ditch was very overgrown, and the hedge neglected, neither having had attention the previous year, and his people had been hard at it all day. He assessed their progress as the day ended, and thoughtfully measured what had still to be done.

"Another four days, I reckon... To get right across."

"Sir." The estimate was acknowledged as probably accurate by Noah Kimber, his labourer, who was working next to him.

Noah had joined the working community that was the Souter farm four years before, as a boy of fourteen. He had come from near London, looking for work, with a history of poverty. They had found him to be hard working and he made himself valuable, so that his initial employment had stretched itself into permanent residence. He was a lightly-built young man, but strong, his body developed by hard labour. He was rather a favourite of the girls, though none as yet had ensnared him, because he observed a famously rigid attitude towards them.

John and Josiah knew why that was; Noah had told them when he arrived, "I judge this to be a godly household, sir. That will suit me well." And indeed, Noah had shown himself well versed in his Bible which, when he arrived, was practically all he possessed. A quotation from Holy Writ was frequently on Noah's lips.

"Whence came this zeal?" Josiah asked once.

"My Ma and Pa are Bible Christians, sir. The whole family are. We are the Kimbers of Stepney village. We even boast a martyr."

"Really?"

"Yes, sir. My mother's great-great-grandmother, sir. Burned by Queen Mary."

"God rest her in glory, then." There was no question thereafter that Noah belonged amongst them.

Now Noah said, "Sir, may I speak with you?"

"Of course. Look, we've done enough for today. Let's walk together." Josiah waited while Noah collected his shaped ditching spade and the pruning hooks. He gathered up the other two workmen and they began the walk, back to the house. Josiah and Noah went together at the rear, and the others drew ahead, out of earshot.

"Well, what do you have to say?" Josiah began.

"Sir, I do say that I am content here. Working here. You and the elder master have been generous to me. And kind masters. I do not want to be judged as ungrateful... "

Josiah had a sinking feeling that he knew what was coming.

Noah rushed on. "But I know that there are great things a-doing in England. We hear about them. We read about them." This last was news to Josiah. *Read*? Where? But Noah was still speaking. "You yourself, sir, we all know, went off to be a part of it. Now, I am a labourer, and it's not for me to go off on a horse, I know. But I can walk. It just seems to me... sir... that what my martyred grandmother died for, it ain't finished, is it? And I can be a part of moving it on, bringing God's Kingdom. Here. Now. And it just seems that God is telling me that I should go and be a part of it. I should be there, standing up and being counted amongst His saints."

This was probably the longest speech that Noah had ever made. Josiah was silent for a moment as they walked, and then said, "So, you want... what?"

"Sir, do you think the saints will have me? Can I join the army of Parliament?"

Josiah stopped and so did Noah. They turned to look at each other. They stood alongside a hedge, and under a huge elm tree, and there was a thrush singing close by.

In his mind's eye, Josiah saw Noah in a red coat. Then he saw, in his imagination, Noah bloodied and pale — dead. The idea was vivid, and he shook his head to throw off the thought. He said, "We should seek the Lord."

And so they stood there, the labourer aspiring to be a soldier, and his employer, the landowner, recently returned from the wars. And after a few moments, Josiah spoke.

"It may not be what you think. It will be hard. It will be *so* hard. You will face danger, mortal danger. You will experience hardship and heart ache. You may be maimed. You may be killed. Consider not going, Noah."

"Oh, I have, sir. I do. But the final part of what God has said to me is this... I can stay here, and part of me says 'yes', that would be good. But I am a labourer, sir. You will look at me and I will always, to you, be a labourer. But sir, if I go away... I will see something of this land, of this world in which God has placed me. I... "

"...you will have an adventure," said Josiah, finishing the thought. He remembered his own motivation in the summer of 1642, when he himself had ridden away from Monks Soham to join Oliver Cromwell. Then he said, "This is what we shall do, Noah. Wait upon the Lord."

"I have so done, sir."

"If, in a week you are still minded to go, then you depart with my blessing — and five pounds conduct money."

"Sir... " Noah was genuinely moved.

"I know that good men are required, Noah. And you are right. It is not over. God's work has not been completed."

It was a nuisance. Good men were also required here in Monks Soham, but there was a cause to defend, to make victorious. It was a cause that they believed God Himself had blessed upon contested battlefields, and it must succeed. People like himself, Josiah knew, must exert themselves to make it succeed. That required sacrifice. One fewer labourer at Monks Soham was the price.

And seven days later, Noah had not changed his mind. And so, his Bible and several pairs of new socks in a knapsack — a gift from the women — he left early one morning to walk into Ipswich, and take the carrier's cart west.

"Go to Windsor. Up the river from London, Noah," Josiah advised him, "Parliament's new army has its base there." Afterwards, Josiah thought to himself that Noah's route would lead him very close to Stepney.

*

So Noah Kimble now stood in his rank, eyes to the front, confident and proud. He was about to be told by his colonel that he was judged competent as a musketeer. They all were.

There were thirty-five men assembled with him. It was a fine day and the field in which they had assembled smelled of new mown grass. Somewhere a blackbird was singing. For a moment, Noah recalled the bird song in Suffolk.

Noah's rank was the second from the front in his file of six men. The file leader, Hezekiah Sedgewick, had become a particular friend, and Noah stood behind him while the four other men of the file were stationed one behind the other to his rear, one long pace apart. At a similar distance, and on his either side were the other files, those men to his own immediate left and right forming his rank. That had been one of his first military lessons: the division of thirty-six musketeers fell into files from front to back, ranks left to right. "Know your position. Get this right," Sergeant Hollin had shouted at them, "and you might get paid as well as killed."

Sergeant Hollin stood now in their front rank, on their right, but with no file behind him and his halberd polished to an unusual brightness.

They were all polished, having been ordered to parade clean, in complete kit, their equipment immaculate, and even laundered shirts. To emphasise the importance of the occasion they had been issued — at last — with their uniform coats, of bright red wool. Noah had never before had a new garment, and, putting it on, he was momentarily overcome with wonder.

"It is a godless colour!" This from Rebecca Marsh, a soldier's wife.

Noah raked his mind. "No, Rebecca. *'The shield of His mighty men is made red, the valiant men are in scarlet'*. The book of Nahum, chapter two. It's the only reference in our Bible to soldiers' coats." He was fairly confident in this assertion. "It is the right colour, the only colour for us."

Moses Marsh said, "Hush woman, Noah is right. It'll keep our spirits high."

"Maybe it is red so's we cannot see when we bleed." This from Mark Golightly, their youngest man — just fourteen. Mark was still very nervous about his new work, but more afeared of Sergeant Hollin than any potential enemy. And he did not know — then — that the red coats *would* show blood, as an ugly black stain.

Their enemy was, anyway, now beaten, according to the scuttlebutt circulating amongst these newly-recruited trainees. "It were Naseby that did it, knocked 'em down," Sergeant Hollin had told them, "and our Oliver is not going to let 'em get up again."

Paul Hollin went in awe of Oliver Cromwell. And why not? Paul had been there, in the press of the infantry combat at Naseby, and felt the shock of Oliver's thundering charge as the Ironsides arrived on the flank of the King's army that day and rolled it away. And now Lieutenant-General Cromwell was not likely to let that malignant army resurrect itself and threaten again England's liberties. "That's where you come in," the sergeant had explained to his command. "We keep those liberties safe!"

So now they stood expectantly, their muskets cleaned to a shine, awaiting their inspection. Hopefully, this would be a formality, for when they had been stood to arms and called into their order, Paul Hollin had walked past each of them slowly, ordering an adjustment there, a refinement here, in order that the credit would be given to them for being "complete" and "correct".

The wind blew through the poplar trees that stood in an almost military line alongside the river. Noah liked looking at that river, because this was Windsor, and the river was the Thames. Noah knew that the river flowed east, down to London, and past his birthplace. He liked to think that any thought he himself had, there beside the water, flowed away downstream, to his parents. But it did not go to Monks Soham.

Sergeant Hollin shouted something unintelligible, and there was a sharp drum roll. "Have a care." In unison, thirty-six expectant musketeers moved their feet, and brought their muskets up to 'rest', barrels pointed up, hands steadily supporting the heavy guns.

Their Colonel walked along their ranks, looking at each man, staring at his face, judging his quality. Noah prayed. First, he asked, *Lord, may I pass muster*, but then, watching Colonel Nathaniel Musgrave, he thought, *He looks at faces, he is not looking at muskets, or bandoliers, but at the man.* This was so, for Nathaniel Musgrave trusted his sergeants to get all things right that achieved 'correctness'. But as he himself had said, "What manner of man we have — that is dictated by the Most High God. It is to that I must direct my own regard. To ask, whether, in the stress of the fight, I may rely upon him."

His Colonel paused before each man, and subjected him to inspection. A few words were passed with some, but not with Noah. He was looked at, then passed over. The men stood stiffly stationary, while the colonel took some time with his assessment. Then Noah saw him come past their right hand file, and take post to their front.

He spoke. "Men. This is the day you pass out and away from your training. You now know your postures. You know well how to make ready your muskets, how to give fire. You know how to do this without peril to your friends, but mortal danger to your enemies. You know of both the potential and the danger of powder. You have mastered your craft."

Yes, indeed. In three weeks, Noah and the others had done nothing else but go through the "postures", the mastery of which made safe the handling simultaneously of burning slow match and deadly black gunpowder. When that was learned, they loaded and fired "ball", lead spheres half an inch round, and so became deadly to their foe. Noah was truly convinced that he could do it all in his sleep. And he was probably right. Colonel Musgrave recalled his attention.

"We have taught you also how to use your sword. God forbid that I catch any one of you using it to chop firewood." There was a smile. "It is there to keep you safe. Remember. In England the wearing of the sword is the mark of a soldier. It is a badge of honour.

"You know too that your strength lies in your moving together, as a body, in your ranks, in your files. You keep together, you move as you have been trained, forwards and back, but always together. You remember that, and you will, I promise you, be irresistible, a terror to your foes. You will never be in danger while you act together, as a body. You know this.

"Above all, you know that the cause in which you have engaged is the cause of the Most High God of Hosts. Has He not shown us upon many fields now that He has blessed this enterprise upon which we are engaged? Aye! Alleluia! Praise Him!" There were murmurs in the ranks echoing the colonel's words. "Be strong in the knowledge that you serve a cause. *The* cause. *The* great cause which is the divine and blessed purpose for this kingdom. You will defend the law, the liberty of the people, their Parliament, and freedom for our faith.

"Have confidence in the Lord of Hosts. Take no glory for yourselves, but attribute all to Him. You are going away from here as soldiers now. Be men who have faith. Be of good courage. Trust in our God. Hold fast to the good cause. Oppose your enemy with a good heart, but protect the weak, the old, the children and all women. Obey your officers. Honour your colours. I truly believe you are a company of saints, a gathered church. So pray. Sing God's praises. Trust always in the Lord!"

He had finished. There was silence. Then Sergeant Hollin shouted, "Huzzah for Colonel Musgrave!" Off came hats, men waved them, as they yelled "Huzzah! Huzzah! Huzzah!"

Musgrave gave them a bow. He acknowledged their quality, doffing his own hat, and smiling.

*

A visitor came to the Souter house in Monks Soham later that year. As an early frost was being burnt away by autumn morning sunshine, a horseman came down the lane and halted his horse in their yard, before stiffly dismounting. He moved as if he was in discomfort. His was a grizzled older face, with the white beard clipped close, but his blue eyes were bright and alert, as if he looked at the world and found it all amusing.

Josiah was just coming out from the kennels, pleased that Hepzebah, the queen of the farm's dogs, had just given birth to a fine litter of pups. His face lit up with new pleasure at the sight of the visitor.

"Isaiah! Isaiah Yates! It does my heart good to see you! Come in. Come in." Josiah was genuinely full of affection. He sat the man down in the parlour and waited upon him as they talked, going himself to fetch small beer and cake.

Isaiah was, for Josiah, a dominant figure from his former life. In Oliver Cromwell's cavalry, Josiah had commanded a troop and Isaiah Yates had been its corporal-of-horse. They had found then that they had much in common, and there had grown between them a warm bond of mutual respect and affection. Isaiah had supported his youthful officer as he found his feet in the military hierarchy. Now, Josiah found himself keen for news of old friends. Isaiah Yates relaxed and gossiped.

"Gideon Beeching? He fell dead at Basing House, so God has taken him into glory. That was another terrible fight. Ahaz Lazenby is still with us, in the Troop, and well, last time I saw him. Praise the Lord. Thomas Woodman is our Captain, has been since Naseby. Maybe he'll take Ahaz as a new Corporal. He deserves it. Make a good 'un. Me? I've had to come home for a bit. I stopped a pistol ball in our last scrap. Surgeon dug it out. That hurt a bit. Knocked me. So, I was sent home on furlough. The Lord has been kind. Three weeks. Came through London from the west, see, and so I thought I'd call upon you.

"At the end, we chased their cavalry all over. Their infantry gave up easy. Came in, surrendered in droves. They all got sent home. But the cavalry were more stubborn. Some of them were *so* stubborn. Always were the better part of the King's army. Mostly quality, I suppose. But can they not see the judgement of God upon the quarrel? Was it not clear? We could see it, why could they not? That man of blood, Charles Stuart, how many more deaths will he make, do you think? Because it is not over yet, is it? We may have tumbled his soldiers, but until the King accepts that things must change, it is not over. This treaty talking goes on and on. London is full of it. Talked of in every tavern...

"The longer it goes on, the more likely it will be that we ourselves divide. I can just see that. Some canting Presbyterian will suddenly work out that he wants King Charles back. The Scots maybe...

"I heard a warning of that. It was when we took the last lot of malignants over in Stow-on-the-Wold, Gloucester way. That's where I stopped the bullet. Probably the last shot of the war. And it hits old Isaiah Yates. Ha! But we got Astley there. Sir Jacob. He was the last of their commanders that anyone would follow. Anyone in their right mind, anyway. One of the best. Old gentleman — 'old', who am I to speak? Old! Ha! Anyway he says — I sees him myself — white hair, white beard, sitting on a drum. At the end. And he says to us, 'Well, gentlemen, it's over'. He says, 'You have done your work'. As indeed we had. Praise God. But then he says, '...you have done your work and you may now go and play. Unless you will fall out amongst yourselves'. *Unless you will fall out amongst yourselves*! What did he mean by that? Eh? May God protect us all."

2. Rumours of War

Isaiah Yates regarded himself as fortunate to have secured a post amongst Oliver Cromwell's staff. Clearly, Oliver, who saw in him a man that had been in the struggle from the start, trusted him. Isaiah was now a galloper: it was his role to deliver Oliver's written instructions. He lived in the Lieutenant-General's personal entourage. He came to know Oliver's intimate colleague, Henry Ireton. He came to know also Colonel Elias Brydon — Oliver's Master of Intelligence — who, some said, had done more for Oliver's success than any other man. They were all frequently together in Westminster, as Oliver fulfilled parliamentary duties, or when he was active in liaison between Parliament and its army. Often too, they were in Windsor, the military base and headquarters.

There was much waiting for instructions. In shifts, the gallopers sat in an outer room, ready, in their buff coats and boots, and armed, prepared to move, while upon the other side of the door lay the room which at that moment constituted Oliver's office. Isaiah passed the time reading. He read anything upon which he could lay his hands, but most frequently he read his Bible.

One November afternoon in Windsor, Oliver emerged from the inner room. As ever, Cromwell was armed, booted and spurred, ready to ride. He did not have, though, his sash or his gorget, the marks of an officer on active duty - which he habitually wore – and his hat was plain and unadorned. As his General emerged from the inner room, Isaiah heard him speak to someone behind, directing his words over his shoulder. He said, "Elias, we will go and see. If you are right, we will find the letter. Get orders to Hammond to close the guard about His Majesty. God forbid that he should slip away now."

Behind Oliver came Commissary-General Ireton. Isaiah saw that Henry Ireton was plainly dressed too, without his own distinctions of rank.

Oliver walked towards an outer door, but beckoned Isaiah Yates as he passed. "Come on Isaiah. We have a job to do."

Isaiah thought, *from their appearance, these two could be just rank-and-file troopers.*

The three of them went out. Horses awaited and they rode off together, taking the road towards London. Cromwell brought his horse alongside Isaiah's mount and spoke to him earnestly.

"Right," said Oliver Cromwell, "Note this, Isaiah. We are, as always, on a mission from the Most High God. But of these next few hours it is important that what we do remains known only to you, I, and the Commissary-General. You understand this?"

"Of course, sir."

"The Commissary-General is convinced that our King Charles is faithless, duplicitous and generally seeking to play a silly game by misleading me, misleading *us*. I am not convinced that this is so. However, Henry..." he slipped into informality "...is now producing proof. We are told that a letter is on its way, a letter that will prove King Charles is seeking to fool us, a letter from himself to the Queen in France." Oliver continued. "We are going to an inn. You will take station outside. Henry and I will be inside. I am sorry, but only *we* will take the ale. Privilege of rank!" He chuckled. "But a man will arrive, carrying a saddle, and when he does, you will inform me. Remember, he will be carrying a saddle. By the Incarnation of Christ, if the King is playing us false, we will make him pay."

After three hours of riding, they were past Charing Cross and heading along Fleet Street towards London City. By now it was dark. They turned through Chancery Lane, past the large houses of the lawyers, with their gardens and smug airs of prosperity.

Cromwell, after giving his instructions, lapsed into silence. Isaiah, taking the hint, had dropped behind, but now Henry Ireton closed with him, "We are three troopers keeping company as equals, mister." So they rode alongside each other. Isaiah remembered that Henry Ireton was a lawyer. He heard a church clock chime, and counted eight.

They came to an inn, and heard the buzz of conversation within. The horses went into the inn's stables, and Isaiah took his station outside, close by the entrance to the back yard, while Cromwell and Ireton went inside. Isaiah, looking in through the window, saw them sit down in a corner, and engage in conversation. A girl came to them, left, and then returned with a pot for each. Isaiah returned his attention to the street. It was dark and apparently empty.

Isaiah looked up at the inn's sign, swinging in a cool light autumn wind. *The Blue Boar*. He stood in the dark at his post wondering whether any man was actually coming. The night was moonless, and he was glad of the solidity of the wall to guard his back. He kept in the shadow inside the yard entrance, and waited. His pulse quickened every time someone approached, but none he saw carried the saddle. Men also emerged from the taproom of *The Blue Boar* and departed into the night. The church clock struck. And again. Ten o'clock.

Then Isaiah saw him. Coming from the city, the east, and carrying upon his head a saddle. Doing this, the man would excite no interest, except that... Oliver had said that he would come. Isaiah watched the man approach, and then turn in at the gate. He waited, unseen in the dark, until the man went into the stable. Then Isaiah went inside the inn. Cromwell rose at his entrance, coming towards him with Ireton at his heels. They went out into the yard, and crossing to the stable, found the man saddling a horse. He had placed the saddle, and the fastening girth hung on either side. Henry Ireton drew his sword.

"Your pardon, mister," said Oliver to the man, "My companions here and I have our orders to search all who leave *The Blue Boar* tonight. But you look an honest fellow, and we will not inconvenience you greatly. Merely, I think, for a moment, relieve you of *this*."

He grasped the saddle and took it to one side, throwing it face down across the stable stall wall, under its single lantern. He felt the lining, moving around the skirt of the saddle and then, apparently finding what he sought, pulled out a small penknife and slit the soft leather.

"What the... ?" protested the man, but Isaiah had hold of his arms.

"Let him go, Isaiah. He knows nothing of this," Oliver said. The man stood there, breathing loudly, without appearing to be about to run, perhaps anxious for his saddle.

Oliver had stood up, and cut open the letter, unfolding it and studying it by the lantern light. Ireton sought to read it too. Oliver then gave the paper to the Commissary-General. Isaiah saw, even in the dim light of that one lantern, the stern expression upon Oliver's face.

"By the Incarnation of Christ, Henry, you were right. He mocks the Lord of Hosts. He cannot see the judgements given in the field." He pointed at the letter. "Bring that. Nothing else."

The Lieutenant-General then strode across to his horse and led it outside. Henry Ireton took his own, and followed.

The man looked at Isaiah. He bleated, "My saddle... "

Isaiah moved his face close and spoke quietly. "Oh, I think you have been very lucky my friend, very lucky. So shut your mouth." Then he took his own horse, and followed the others. By the time he caught up they were already into Holborn and heading away west, towards Windsor.

*

Noah Kimber and his companions, with all of Musgrave's regiment, some 800 men, had marched out of Windsor the day after that parade of the thirty-six musketeers judged to be competent. Those men had replaced losses from the regiment's strength, for Musgrave's was one of the army's veteran regiments.

It went with drums beating and flags flying, uniformed in the red coats, and took the road west. Their officers aimed for twenty-five miles each day. "A saunter," Sergeant Hollin called it, "ye'r still soft. When we're with the army, we'll only do ten miles a day, if we're lucky. Can't go faster than the big guns and bread wagons, see. But when it's just us — just Musgrave's — we'll do twenty-five, because we are the fucking *best*. We shoot straight and we march fast. Faster than any other bastard regiment. So, step out lively and stop grumbling."

Noah was shod in heavy shoes, their soles reinforced with thick nails. Within, his feet wore wool stockings, over which were linen over-socks. Their feet were inspected each evening by the ever-vigilant Sergeant Hollin, who issued dollops of goose grease — "only the best for Musgrave's men!" — which, he promised, would harden the feet of his new men. By the third day, both feet were tender at the heel, but Noah found to his surprise that from that day forward the discomfort diminished. "Told you so," said his Sergeant, "now you will do what soldiers do — walk the length of the bloody country in six weeks for sixpence a day. And you thought soldiering would be fighting!"

On such marches, 'in the field' as it was styled, each file lived together. The closeness of the team was made by the bonding of familiarity, through eating, sleeping and being continually in close proximity to each other.

Noah found his family in the men of his file. Even their eccentricities, perhaps irritating at the start, came, first to be a source of banter, and then, without realising that he was crossing a barrier, accepted with love. After their time of training together, the march completed the bond. And after still further time together, Noah, although he might not have been able to say so, would instinctively place himself in danger, if, by doing so, he could save the life of one of the others. This, of course, was precisely what his officers — and the Parliament — wanted.

So the six men of the file became a unit, bonded for the fight.

Six men plus Rebecca. She earned pennies darning and replacing buttons and made their morning porridge. Noah saw that she was devoted to her man. The couple had scant privacy, and whatever conjugality they enjoyed, they risked it being both overheard and seen. No-one took any liberties with Rebecca; Moses Marsh had the look of a prize-fighter and she was secure in his protection. She also had the rest of the file as close neighbours. They had now become her man's family and she was embraced within it.

As they moved, Rebecca walked behind the regiment, followed the camp, and she was not the only woman to do so.

Recognising their inexperience, Colonel Musgrave had his new musketeers put through their "postures" at the end of each day's march. This concluded with live firing, with lit match and ball.

Noah had mastered his craft. In training each of the postures was distinctly and separately ordered and then implemented, but now, since they were judged competent, the only words given to them were "Make ready!"

Noah found himself always ahead when the next word came: "*Pre...sent!*" At this the front rank muskets came up, butts pressed to the shoulder, muzzle pointing forward, awaiting the final order of the process: "*Give Fire!*"

"Three shots a minute. From each of you. That's what we are aiming for," Sergeant Hollin confided.

It was always satisfying when a rank fired together, a crashing bang, the loudest noise ever to echo in many of the rural spots in which they camped. They always smiled as, after it, the rooks rose cawing above them, or deer or rabbits revealed themselves by rising and running. But the overwhelming requirement of them was moving, marching, hour after hour, day after day. Noah became tough: his legs came to ache less, his shoulders to hurt less from the weight he carried, biscuit, knapsack and musket. As he looked at his hands he saw them grow brown with the summer sun, and he saw in comrades' faces the tanning that was on his own.

He also sang. The regiment had a wonderful collective voice, and all of them had grown up singing Psalms in their churches. This moving column of committed men was motivated by a strong religious zeal, and a conviction that they were here, in this army, to safeguard the freedom to worship as they wished. They gave expression to this in spontaneous singing, and chose the Psalms as a truly democratic mechanism, whereby a soul shouted its freedom from the bigoted control of king or priest. Noah joined in with enthusiasm.

The regiment had its drums, and their beats tapped the step when, wearied with the day, their stride flagged. But Nathaniel Musgrave had also endowed his men with two fifers, and these could be relied upon to strike up in support of any singing.

They passed Reading, and went up into the rolling downland of Berkshire, where the chalk dust rose around them from the highway, and the vanguard saw skylarks ascend from the surrounding fields. Outside Newbury they camped beside the Kennett, before passing through the town, south of the fields that had seen two stiffly contested fights in the late war, and so on to Hungerford and Marlborough. A Sunday rest was spent outside Chippenham before they spent two days halted four miles outside Bristol. They relaxed near Lansdowne Hill, the site of another battle, but no one went to look. Noah was so tired that he only emerged from the tent to eat and serve his duties in the picquets. Besides, as Sergeant Hollin pointed out, "I think the King got the best o' that one."

Then the scuttlebutt was all talk of their destination, Bristol.

Nathaniel Musgrave had spent the journey riding at the head of them, out of sight of Noah, save when Noah's file went out on point. That had occurred four times, and on those occasions, Noah's file was sent some quarter of a mile ahead of the regiment. They had to run, "to double" up to the front, where their function was to march ahead, to draw out any ambush. No such unpleasantness occurred. But Colonel Musgrave became visible then to Noah, since they had to go past both him and the regiment's field officers to take the exposed leading position. They swept off their hats in salute and their Colonel acknowledged their homage.

Hezekiah Sedgewick took the opportunity then to remind them that they were in Parliament's new modelled army. "You saw that? That's the thing about this army. A salute. Our commander really thinks we are worth something. Eh?" And apparently he did. A smile had played on Musgrave's face. Noah liked the man. Not a bad start.

Noah again would have had trouble finding the words to express it, but *The New Model*, as history calls it, was a new thing. Its chief quality was discipline, but that discipline was created not by fear of punishment, but by the quality of what the soldiers themselves experienced from their leaders. That spirit was the work of three men: Thomas Fairfax, Phillip Skippon and Oliver Cromwell.

Three-eighths of Musgrave's regiment were pikemen, armed with 18-foot-long staves tipped with steel. Their job was to hold the ground won from the enemy, and they wore a steel helmet, and back and breast plates. Pikemen regarded themselves as the superior arm, though Noah was never sure why.

For their entry into Bristol, Musgrave divided his command into three, placing his musketeers to front and rear of his pikemen, who themselves had at their centre the regiment's Ensigns carrying their colours, the flags which were the honour of them all.

So they came into the city.

*

Isaiah Yates had rather enjoyed his escapade with his two generals. Intriguing as it was, that secret visit to *The Blue Boar* in Holborn was never spoken of by him to any man. He had grasped the significance of the visit — Isaiah was no fool — but what use the two commanding personalities of militant Independency would make of that night's discovery, for the moment remained hidden.

It was not unconnected with what happened to Isaiah next. He was promoted to become a Cornet, and in this junior officer rank, he found himself coming into the circle of Colonel Elias Brydon.

Elias Brydon headed up the first-class intelligence service that supported Parliament's new modelled army. Brydon's "business", as they styled it, was older than the army itself, for Oliver Cromwell, when only a Troop Captain, had quickly realised the need for good information, and as Commander of the Horse of the Eastern Association, he (and Brydon) had built up a formidable apparatus. When he later became the new army's Lieutenant-General, Cromwell brought with him Brydon's people and their skill. It had all worked brilliantly. Now, a network of observant people, supported by a web of couriers, gathered information nation-wide. It faithfully reported where there remained any nest of recalcitrant royalists, feeding to the army's leaders the intelligence they required to snuff out the last embers of civil war. If some fugitive Royalist captain, desperately casting about for the wherewithal to strike back, found himself suddenly surrounded by Cromwell's troopers, it was because Elias Brydon's people had tracked him down. If Corfe Castle fell to a *ruse de guerre* — as it did — then Brydon's people had supplied the information that enabled the trick. When Lathom House fell it was because the secrets of its defence were known to Elias Brydon's spies. In this way Brydon's "business" was making a major contribution to the success of the army's conquest. It allowed limited resources to be effectively targeted.

The fighting of the civil war had died away, and pacification became the goal, but far from seeing the winding down of Brydon's small empire, the times called for it to be newly invigorated. The continual chicaneries of the duplicitous king had to be countered, and the activities of his partisans blocked.

There was more. Elias Brydon was as committed to the need for religious freedom as any man in Oliver's regiments. The high command of the army — the Grandees — had further struggle before them if they must win the peace.

Oliver Cromwell said later that, whatever made men first fight for or against King Charles, in the end what divided them was religion. It was not that they were quarrelling about the truths of Christianity, as those were accepted by the vast majority. What was fought over was the government of the church, and in particular whether men were to have their belief dictated to them, or whether a state could exist when allowing within itself differing ecclesiastical polities. Until men went to war, England had a national church, policed by the King and its bishops, and tracing its lineage back through mediaeval times, when it was subject to the Pope. This situation was the creation of King Henry VIII, who had replaced the Pope with himself. But now men were asking to be free, and, this King Charles denying them freedom, men had come out fighting. The experiment had to be made, that within the one state there could be many ecclesiastical structures. This was what the army now fought for. And its opponents continued to say that the nation must be of one faith, and one order, and that all men must submit. One group that had said as much had now been tumbled: King Charles and his Cavalier Church of England. Now the army found itself faced with another group: the Presbyterians. The Presbyterian system would involve a national church, prescribed belief, government by presbyters, and persecution of dissents: it paraded itself as such in Scotland. Sadly, English soldiers heard it advocated by some members of the Parliament they served. Presbyterian supremacy, whether English or Scots, this army would resist. Its own watchword was tolerance, its preferred church system was locally "gathered communities" of believers, each independent of the next, choosing their Ministers and with no overarching connection. "Independents" became the label for those holding this opinion.

At this moment — and Isaiah came to grasp this from overheard conversations — the Grandees saw a very real threat to a peaceful settlement of the nation. That threat was the imposition upon it of the Presbyterian system, perhaps by King Charles in a new alliance with those members of the Parliament, and perhaps by the intervention of the Scots.

So, Elias Brydon had to adjust his focus, and to shift his game. He had to deploy the "business" to look into what the Scots were up to, and even to keep the army's eye upon certain parliamentarians, while not neglecting those last few embers of Royalist fire that continued to glow in the ashes of King Charles' following. Brydon was a man of great capacity, and served by talented people — how else could Tom Fairfax and Oliver Cromwell achieve what they had? But even he felt the stress.

A loud "By the Incarnation of Christ, Elias!" was heard in the outer waiting room, one day. It was Lieutenant-General Oliver Cromwell's voice. "If you need more people, we must get them. We will find the money. Somewhere. I *must* know." The voice dropped, and there was no more to be heard, but the waiting gallopers looked at each other. Eyebrows were raised.

Then the door opened and Oliver came out. He looked at the room. He said, turning back, "Look, there's three men here: intelligent, crafty — what was it you said they must be?" He was laughing. Then, "See if any of them will work for you. There's Isaiah here. He will serve. Make him an officer. He deserves it."

That was how Isaiah Yates, without seeking it, was promoted to be a Cornet, holding the Parliament's commission, and entered Elias Brydon's "business", becoming one of Oliver Cromwell's 'intelligencers'. He was vaguely aware that his one-time Troop Commander, Josiah Souter, had some knowledge of Brydon's work, and he resolved to ask him about that experience when they next met. But for now, he settled down into learning all he could from those who were nearer.

3. 1648

Two years passed. John Souter was able to view with equanimity the developments within his little world. His son appeared completely restored. Beginning on that night he had found himself able to talk, Josiah's old interest and energy had revived. He took a larger and larger share of responsibility for their land and its people. The older man found himself in the novel position of strolling over his place with time upon his hands.

Josiah found himself embracing the role for which he was apparently destined, increasingly absorbed in the daily round of decisions and activity which the seasons brought to Suffolk farming. It was a full and busy life, with satisfying demands upon his body and mind. He saw the farm's profitability begin to climb away from the depressed years imposed by England's troubles, and he took satisfaction in the achievement. It was remarkable that this occurred, because it was against a national trend. The harvest was poor in each of the two years immediately after the war. He became aware of a struggle for prosperity in the lives of the neighbours he met at market, and heard tales of hardship in more distant parts. But Josiah, fully absorbed in the task and focussed on management of his own farm, felt more and more light-hearted. In these happier circumstances, days began to come and go without any hurtful recollection of his time in Oliver Cromwell's cavalry.

Except that when he saw Phoebe, he remembered Praisegod.

And when he saw Susanna...

Susanna and he had first met when she was destitute and recently widowed, in the harsh winter of 1643. He had sent her, and her son Charlie, to his own home to find shelter and work. But now Susanna was so changed that before long he failed to find any painful memory. She had blossomed with her new life. She was beautiful, her dark eyes still so striking, in a face full of grace and cheerfulness. What Josiah felt when he did meet her was entirely a novelty. It was becoming troublesome to his heart and mind.

If Susanna realised the effect she had upon Josiah, she gave no sign of it. Phoebe, however, who was always alert in her observations of people, saw it quickly. She did not speak of it to either party, but smiled, noted it and kept it, for the moment, to herself. The two women had struck up a friendship. They had in common that they were both seen as Royalist partisans in a household committed to Parliament. There was never any animosity, but rather everyone else extended sympathy. Actually, neither Susanna, widowed by the fighting, nor Phoebe, who had lost her employer and friend, cared much for King Charles or his fortunes. They laughed about it. And it was in the sharing of that joke that their mutual liking grew.

One other person had noticed Susanna's effect upon Josiah. His father too had seen it. When Josiah had first returned from soldiering, John had seen the embarrassment of his son when finding Susanna there. Old John himself had a real soft spot for Susanna, with her lilting Monmouth accent and those almond-shaped eyes. He could think of no one he would rather have as his daughter. John was isolated in his farming life upon his own land, and encounters with his social peers were rare, so that his world was there, his day-to-day conversations with those around him, amongst his own household and on his farm. Perhaps as a result, he would have queried any suggestion that his son was too grand for Susanna, or that she was his social inferior. Such considerations of status he seemed to have outgrown. He thought he saw love. He understood that because he shared it.

Charlie, now nine years old, worked in the Souters' stable. As far as Josiah could judge, the boy was happy. He appeared bright, cheerful and willing. Within the stables, he came under the patriarchal control of an old man, Ebenezer, whose province they were.

No one had ever recorded Ebenezer's birth, parentage or origin, so all knew him simply by that one name. But everyone acknowledged that there was very little that old Ebenezer did not know about horses. For each of the beasts in his care he had the love of a father to his child, and to his mind their welfare was the supreme consideration. To others, who might see in a horse a mere exploitable resource, Ebenezer directed a fierce aggressive vehemence. Many went therefore in fear of him. But the old man had found room in his heart for Charlie, and had set out to pass on to the boy all his equine knowledge and much else, not excluding the recipes for the ointments and poultices with which he treated the cuts, bruises and sprains inevitable on hard-worked farm beasts. Ebenezer had even set the broken leg of the horse being ridden by John Souter in that accident that lamed him.

One intriguing eccentricity of Ebenezer was that he never used the poleaxe. When, as happened occasionally but inevitably, through accident or disease, a horse had to be 'made mincemeat', as they said, Ebenezer always used an ancient gun. This carried on its still functioning dog-lock the date *1603*, and Ebenezer always called it "My Queen" and reminded everyone that the date of the gun's making saw also the death of Good Queen Bess. "Now, that year," said Ebenezer, who was perhaps twenty-five years old at that time, "was the last time God smiled on England." This was a somewhat enigmatic comment, as John Souter once pointed out. On that occasion, Ebenezer had merely smiled, and spat, so none was really the wiser. All wondered: did God smile, in Ebenezer's view, because the great Queen had at last died, or had he been continuously smiling throughout the forty years of her reign, and ceased to do so when that Scottish clown James Stuart followed her to the throne?

One who was allowed without hindrance into Ebenezer's kingdom was Josiah, for the old man knew that his young master too had a love of his horses. Most of all, Josiah loved Judgement, the bay stallion he had ridden off in the summer of 1642 when he had joined Oliver Cromwell's cavalry. Together they had gone through much, not excluding Oliver's manoeuvres that had won Marston Moor. Often, Josiah himself brushed Judgement's glossy back and flanks, and combed out his tail and mane. And often too, as he did this, Ebenezer set Charlie to work on Judgement's legs. As they worked together, Josiah wanted so much to begin a conversation, but found that he could not — at least not with any ease. The two were therefore used to working in silence.

One day Josiah finally found his voice. He asked, "Do you remember your father, Charlie?"

"No, sir. Not much. Odd things. Like the smell of leather."

Josiah smiled. Yes, leather gave off so many different scents. Which depended upon its use, on horses, on men, whatever. And the smell brought memories. Of people, often. Josiah paused to get a particular tangle out of Judgement's forelock. "Steady, old friend, hold still," he was talking to his horse. Then, "Was your father a horseman?"

"No, sir. He were a forester. That much I do remember."

"Not in the cavalry then?"

"No, sir. He were a sergeant in a foot regiment. That I know too."

Josiah absorbed this. A forester was a skilled and respected man, probably employed by some landowner, given the use of a tied cottage, the right to catch his meals, and not much else. But even without much, he would command respect amongst his fellow workers, by virtue of his knowledge and skill, his craft. This would command some value too in his employers' estimation. So, gaining a sergeant's rank followed.

"Can you polish Judgement's hooves, Charlie?" Josiah was not in the business of grilling the boy. But he said, "Do you have your letters?"

"My mother is teaching me, sir."

"That's good, Charlie. Keep at it. A man needs to know the secret of reading and writing. It will serve you well." Josiah turned his attention to Judgement's mane. This covered his inability to frame further conversation. It was Charlie who broke the silence.

"Sir. Was my father wrong to go and fight? For King Charles, I mean?"

"Is that what he did, Charlie? Do you think he went off purposefully to kill and perhaps to die for a king? Or did he go because someone closer to you all made him go? Many of the soldiers were made to become so by their landlords, their employers. Who did he work for?"

"I don't know, sir."

"You need to ask your mother. But Charlie, even if he chose to go, that's nothing to be ashamed of."

"You did not though, sir, did you? Go and fight for the King."

"No. I did not."

Josiah saw for a moment the boy's perplexity. The youngster wanted to admire and remember his father. But Charlie knew that the Souter household, in which the child had found such comfort, was opposed to what his father had died defending.

"Was it an easy choice, sir?"

Josiah stopped work and leaned for a moment upon Judgement's flank. He remembered.

"I did think... I might be a rebel — against the law. We all did. But we had to obey a higher law. We wanted to stop what was happening, things we thought the King was doing that were wrong, and... we wanted to make other things happen that he was not going to do unless we made him."

Charlie asked, "And did you? Did you stop him? Make things happen?"

There was a long pause. Josiah realised that Charlie had put into a brief question, all the unhappiness that was in his — Josiah's — mind. Then Judgement moved, made uncomfortable by Josiah's elbow resting too long upon his ribs.

"Charlie, it is too soon to tell." He laughed, and it was bitter. Despite it all, all the death, all the effort, all the destruction, King Charles was still the King. England was apparently unchanged. But then, *no*, he thought, *we won*. England would never be the same again. He was right. It was too soon to tell.

Then he thought more. Yes, we no longer have bishops. We no longer have those awful church courts. The result of their abolition had rather tended to make the church in England chaotic, but in Monks Soham the wider situation was not apparent. Here, their vicar, the Reverend Endsleigh Seaton, continued to deliver his three-hour sermons on Sundays in a church devoid of all ornament, confident in the support of his squire and patron, the elder Souter.

Josiah was working with the brush again. He thought Charlie should be told more. He said, "There is a treaty being discussed, between the King and the Parliament. They are trying to resolve the issues that divided us."

"But the King is beaten, sir. The war is over. Can't the Parliament just say how it is going to be? Hasn't God told King Charles that he's wrong?"

"Spoken like an Ironside, Charlie. Yes. We think God has spoken to us. In the Parliament's victory."

"Especially at Naseby, sir. Because the Parliament's infantry were such novices. Ebenezer told me that. Were you there, sir?"

"No, Charlie. I had been sent off on another piece of work. But Oliver was there." Josiah stopped again as he recalled Oliver Cromwell sending him off on the eve of Naseby. With Praisegod.

"Oliver? Oliver Cromwell, sir?"

"Aye. Oliver Cromwell. He was our captain. A great soldier. A great man."

"Will he be doing this treaty then, sir?" Charlie was genuinely interested.

"I do hope so, Charlie. I hope so."

"What's he like then, this Cromwell?"

"He has a great heart, Charlie. A great heart. Now, come on Charlie, we must finish the job. Judgement has been fussed over long enough."

Ebenezer had come proprietarily into the stall, thinking probably that Charlie was delaying completion of Judgement's grooming. "Now sir, is this youngster talking instead of working? Eh? Lord, but he likes to talk. Don't you, young Charles?" The old man put his arm around Charlie's shoulders. Josiah could see unfeigned affection in the gesture.

He said, in mock reproach, "Ebenezer! When we are young, that's how we find out about the world. By talking."

"That's as maybe, master. But talking don't get Judgement groomed, do it?"

There was no argument against the logic of this, except that Josiah thought that Judgement had rather enjoyed being in the centre of the conversation, but he forbore to put this forward as an argument, knowing that Ebenezer would find little merit in it. Instead he handed over the brush to Ebenezer, and made to go, saying, "You finish him then, Ebenezer. It must nearly be time for dinner. And Charlie, don't forget to speak to your mother."

When Josiah had gone, Ebenezer said to his young apprentice, "And what must you remember to ask your mother, Charlie?"

"I am to ask about my father. Why he went to be a soldier. Out for the King."

"And will you Charlie? Will you ask?"

"Yes. I suppose I must."

"Yes, Charlie, you must. If the master gives you any instruction, you do it. You do it." He poked the brush in Charlie's direction.

Ebenezer noted, but kept to himself for now, Josiah's interest in the matter.

Except that, in Phoebe's kitchen, to which Ebenezer reported each bed time for his nightcap, he said to her, "Young Charlie has been told by Master Josiah to ask of his mother about his father."

Phoebe had said, "And why do you think that was so?"

Ebenezer had no spoken answer to this, except that he looked at Phoebe. She was smiling. He began to understand.

4. Prelude

Charlie did speak to his mother. He did this rather because he was now under an obligation to do so, rather than from curiosity. He had no wish to rake up sadness from his mother's past.

It was one evening, and he had just finished his reading. Only one text was at hand. It was the Bible. By coincidence, the passage Susanna had been guiding her young son through had been the passage in Genesis, where the patriarch Abraham had failed to sacrifice his own son, the child of promise. He had done so because God had revealed to him that human death had no part in worship.

"It is an old, old story, Charlie. And ever since, we have known that the service of the true God has no requirement for death. Before it, they did not always think like that."

"Did Isaac love his father? After that?"

"I think he served him well. But we will read about that as we continue tomorrow."

So Charlie asked about his own father.

Susanna said, "You ought to know about your father, Charlie. He was a good man. He was a person of integrity. He cared for you." His mother's soft voice, with her Monmouth accent, was good to hear. He had not heard her talk a lot lately, he realised.

"Did he care about King Charles?" That was the nub of Charlie's interest.

Susanna thought about her response for a moment.

"You are wondering whether he acted from conviction. That affects your peace of mind here, in this household. Well, Charlie, I think your father went off a-soldiering because he was looking for an adventure. He was looking for a different life. He worked on an estate, see, and the man who employed him took all his workers off to join King Charles."

"He had to go, then?"

"Mm… no. Because some of them deserted and came home pretty quickly. But perhaps yes, because, for those other fellows, coming home cost them their employment. But, Charlie, we are now working here for

Mister Souter. He has not acted badly towards us because of your father's actions. Rather the reverse. Both of the masters have been kind. We are fortunate. Let us look to the future, Charlie. Let us say thank you to Mister Souter in the best way we can. By working well."

"They will not expect me to go and fight, will they?"

"Ah. I hope not. I do not think that they would. Anyway, the young Mister Souter has not gone off, has he? If you mean would they make you fight for King Charles, I think that is definitely not."

"But what about the Parliament?"

"I think the Parliament can manage without you, Charlie. It seems, from what I have heard, that it is doing mighty well without you. Or Josiah. Thank the Lord." Charlie did not detect the catch in his mother's throat at the mention of their younger master's name, nor see her eyes.

"I would not want to fight for King Charles."

"No. I would not want you to either, my dear one. What has King Charles done for you and I? Mm?"

"I think he killed my father."

"Yes. I suppose he did. He had all that power, but he could not govern his kingdom so that people could live in peace. That is a great failure. A terrible failure. A betrayal, really. Of trust."

"I hate him."

"Hate is a terrible thing too, Charlie. Hate no one. Now, it is late, and Ebenezer will want you to work early tomorrow. Was there not talk of a visit to the smithy?"

Charlie obediently went off to his bed above the stables. He was a little better informed.

Susanna, however, found the recollections raised by her son's questions deeply unsettling. Why? Because, she realised, she had now become utterly devoted to Josiah. The realisation seemed to warm her, but at the same time bring her a sharp pang, as if anticipating grief. She was a worker in his house. He was a master, who was separated from her by a great divide of status.

Besides, she had no reason to think that he saw in her anything worthy of his attention. It was a dream. She found herself weeping; in loneliness, in a feeling of not being loved. Recollection of her past love meant she knew what was missing, what was real. She realised that she was weeping with grief for loss, with longing, with love for a man she could never have.

Susanna was a woman of some self-discipline and strength, and after a while she rose, wiped her hand across her eyes, and went into the kitchen to be with Phoebe.

Phoebe could see that she had wept, but since Ebenezer was present, enjoying his evening posset, nothing except a look passed between the two friends to mark the hurt. Instead, Susanna's face broke into a smile and she joined in the conversation with a forced jollity.

Later, when the old man had left for his bed, the two women sat alone in the candlelight. Phoebe said, "what had upset you earlier?"

"Loss," said Susanna. "And loneliness. And longing."

"I think that there is a cure for all your sadness of heart. You need a new love."

"I have a new love, Phoebe. In the sense of me feeling love towards someone. Trouble is, it is for the wrong man."

"Ha! Why wrong?"

"Well, 'tis hopeless. Is it not?" Susanna made no explanation. If she was surprised that Phoebe knew her secret, she did not say so. She took it as understood that her friend should know what was hiding in her heart.

"You think it is so. And while you think it is so, it may continue to be so. But here is an alternative. Look to him, look at him, speak to him. You know how approachable he is. He's always around the place, available."

"Available?"

"Yes, I mean we often see him, pass him in the house or the yard. He always greets us, don't 'ee? Yes. And what do you do? Oh, I know, Susanna, you look at the ground. You probably blush. Look, my dear. You have an advantage."

"How so?"

"How many wenches do you think Josiah Souter has bedded? Eh? Him in his puritan suit?" They laughed. "Yes. And you, you see, have the advantage... "

"Of experience?"

"Yes. Exactly. Now, we are going to use that."

"*We?*"

"Oh aye! I'm not going to be left out of this!"

*

If Josiah had known what was being plotted in the kitchen of his own house, he might at that moment have been less relaxed. But it was a late summer evening, and, having completed their daily inspection of their property, he and his father were taking an evening bottle of wine while absorbed in a conversation.

"We ought to pay seven pence a day for a labourer." There were concerns about wage levels: local employers were saying that men were scarce. Good men scarcer still.

"It was always so," said John, "but the war has made it worse." As the magistrate, he had to fix the local wage rate.

Josiah helped him. "We can afford it. Look, we are getting three pounds a quarter for our wheat."

John, as always seeing the point of view of the poor, said, "Dear God. Mercy. Bread will be so expensive."

"So give the labourer seven pence."

"Money is going out of the county, Josiah, at a fantastic rate. The county committee is at work relentlessly. We need to settle that demand they sent us."

"We will, father. Blame bloody King Charles. Him, and his inability to see God's will. Nationally, over half of a million pounds goes on the army each year. Our army. Did you know that? Just to keep the peace."

"Dear Lord. That's a swingeing lot of money. I had not thought to praise the London financiers. Not before they so mightily placed their interests at the service of our Parliament. But they are doing it, aren't they? Funding it. Them and these sequestrations."

Josiah said, "I think sequestration is right. It is imposed upon those who broke the peace. We would not question..."

"Josiah," his father was unconvinced, "if you remember it was not them that broke the peace. You and I were anxious less, after the event, we be judged rebels. Remember?"

"Those who resisted should pay the cost. Of all the war and damage. The precedent is there. Traitors always lost their estates, their property."

"Aye. When a court found that they as individuals were guilty. As individuals."

"Father! Was Walter Raleigh guilty? You always told me that his execution was a political farce."

"No. You argue falsely. I only mean that the party with the power decides who is and who is not guilty. Who *was* not guilty rather, for it is after the event. Long after."

"Long after God showed His will, Father. If the fortunes of war had gone otherwise, it might be us that were facing sequestration. Or worse."

"But it did not..."

"No. God in His mercy decreed otherwise. Anyway, they have to take an oath."

"And then lose their income." John was adamant. He sensed that the matter was fundamentally unjust.

"Not all of it. If the malignant concerned was, before the war, a member of the Parliament, it is half. For others it is as low as one-sixth. And a wife and children get one-fifth."

"Generous! Well, Matthew Cribbins is losing two years income. *Two years*, Josiah. So all his men and their children go hungry." The old man was genuinely concerned. Matthew Cribbins was a neighbouring landowner.

Josiah scoffed. "And he has lost his right to nominate the parson. You always said that he was a covert papist. Anyway, this has been going on now for four years. Why bring it up now?"

"Because I am alerted to Matthew Cribbins' position. Two of his men were here looking for work today. He had discharged them. I had to send them away. They said they would look for work by joining the army."

"The army is recruiting for Ireland."

"Oh Aye! Ireland. Chaotic as ever. Plenty of horrid work there. Why cannot the English leave Ireland in peace? Scotland is not much better." John gave Josiah a news-sheet.

Josiah looked through it for a moment. Then he said, "Oh look! No lay preaching. Parliament says so. That's a Presbyterian rule if ever I saw one. A rule worthy of a papist! The army will ignore it. Did I ever tell you, Father, I used to preach the Word to my troop..." For a moment, Josiah was silent, remembering. One Christmas sermon stood out, because... of course, because immediately after it he had first seen Susanna.

"Your mother," said John, "would have been proud of you."

From the front page of the news-sheet, Josiah read that the Parliament's army had decided for itself that it was a power in the land, *'for we speak for the people of England, and the people are the source of power'.*

"The people are the source of power," he said out loud.

"What was that?" asked his uncomprehending father.

"The people are the source of power. I had not thought thus about political power in this kingdom. But it is so, isn't it?"

"It is?"

"Yes. For if a king struts across the land, what is it that keeps him there? Is it not the unremitting labour and craft of countless thousands of humble people, who work, make wealth and pay their tax into his coffers. And the more of them, and the more tax, the greater the King. So, the people, yes, they are the source of power. It is well said."

"Is that your Mister Cromwell?"

"I rather think it is my Mister Ireton. But it is a sentiment that Oliver would share. As do I. And you I think. We thought that the Parliament represents the people. I fought for it because it does."

"It represents only those, I think, who vote in its elections. Not Matthew Cribbins' labourers," his father ventured, adding, "...his *ex*-labourers."

"No, that's where this statement by the army agrees with your thinking. For Matthew's men will shortly be trailing a pike or working a musket in the army, and therefore..."

"The army represents the people..."

"Better than a Parliament elected by their employers and the rich men."

"I see," said the older man, beginning to feel more uneasy at the revolutionary implications of the revelation. "What else is there?"

Josiah continued studying the news-sheet. "It says that the Parliament must dissolve. That's only right, father, they've sat long enough. The army wants an election every two years, I think. Is that what 'bi-ennial' means? Can't mean an election every six months, no. A parliament can only last for eight months. They want a remodelling — I like that word, 'remodel', like the army itself! Remodel the constituencies and the franchise. Great and gracious God, that's ambitious. Considering the challenge to vested interests..."

"It seems they have an aversion to their current employers."

"You can imagine, father. The men that have directed the Parliament's affairs since, when? Thirty-eight? And still there. They will have made fortunes."

"So, turn 'em out. Start again. That's good."

Josiah quoted again, "*Now we must remodel the institutions of the Kingdom to safeguard us against usurpation, against arbitrary powers.* Yes, that's good. They propose a council of state, for the Kingdom's better government, any decision for peace or war."

"That was always the King's prerogative."

"Not any more. And — you'll like this — Parliament is to choose the officers of the militia."

"Ha!" The older man laughed. That matter had been amongst the first on which England had divided.

"But father, look at this!" Josiah was genuinely excited. "The army wants tolerance of all faiths. Tolerance, that's not freedom of religion, but it's going in the right direction. *No coercive power in the church... No Prayer Book... No obligation to worship in our parish church.* Yes! *No solemn league and covenant'.* Yes! Yes! Praise the Lord! Huzzah!" He shouted. "Huzzah! Huzzah!"

"Steady, Josiah. It isn't law yet."

Phoebe had entered the room, followed by Susanna, wide eyed and enquiring.

"Why do they tell us all this now?' asked John. "Phoebe?"

"We wondered if all was well, sir. The noise... "

"My son was excited by some news Phoebe. All is well."

Josiah was standing looking out through the windows at the darkness. In his pleasure at the news he was trembling, but in the dark window he could see the reflection of the room, his father, the two women.

Susanna, standing just inside the door, was holding a candle.

Josiah looked at her and suddenly knew that what he wanted most of all — even more than toleration for England's religions — was Susanna.

*

"I am watching for Scotland, Isaiah. We need to keep our eyes on Berwick. And Carlisle. Apparently Marmaduke Langdale is sulking up in the Cheviots. He's never won a fight yet, so I can't say it frightens me, but why is he there? The malignants in the south are waiting. They are waiting for the Scots."

Colonel Elias Brydon was looking at a great map of England that he had nailed upon the wall of his office in Windsor. He had hit upon the novel idea of banging pins into it, with little paper flags attached, bearing names. Each flag was a potential point of interest. There were concentrations of the flags at several points; at Carlisle, at Berwick certainly, but also in Wales. A cause of greater anxiety to him were other flags however, pinned into the map at Maidstone, Colchester and London.

Isaiah thought that Colonel Elias Brydon looked exhausted. Isaiah had become very close to his Colonel. Brydon sat, his face in his hands, elbow on his desk. He said, "*By the Incarnation of Christ*, as Oliver would say! The whole dreadful business could start again." He picked up a paper from his desk.

"No, Colonel. It is not as it was."

"How so?" Brydon looked up.

"First, because we can see what is occurring. You *know* of Poyner's treachery. You will tell others. Something will be done. Second, we have the army now. Thirdly, Oliver is in control."

"Yes," said Brydon, cheering up. "But you are right, Isaiah." He looked again at the paper he had been handling. "We must first close off Pembroke. If Irish troops come in through there, Wales may give the malignants resources that... that we must deny them."

They both knew that Oliver Cromwell had been ill, seriously ill. The question in their minds, thus far unspoken, was whether he was yet fit enough to take the field.

The news they had gathered, not two days old, was that Pembroke — with its port and its strong Castle — might be on the verge of becoming a royalist stronghold. Its governor, its Parliamentary governor, Colonel John Poyer, intended to refuse orders, and somehow decide that his allegiance was after all to King Charles. "What a man of *honour* his majesty has acquired to serve him," Elias Brydon said sarcastically, for he knew Poyer. "Such a proper arsehole."

The information had come by pigeon. This was another of Elias Brydon's innovations, an experiment in military communication. Homing pigeons, each with a tiny container for messages attached to a leg. Two pigeons had arrived in the loft at Windsor; their informant wished to make sure by doubling the chance of the message arriving. The news would be repeated via a human courier later that week. Meantime, Brydon said, "I will go and report this at once. I believe that the Lord General considers that he has fully recovered, although I'm not sure the doctors agree."

"He will want to be off, when he sees that."

"Yes," Brydon rejoined and picking up his hat, he went out.

Isaiah went back to the sheaf of papers the two of them had been studying when the message from southwest Wales had been handed over. He looked carefully looked at what was before him, placing each message within a chronological sequence, and seeking to ascertain where in the land it had come from.

He had also to hand a coded letter, and leaving the papers sorted upon his colonel's desk, retreated to his own and began to decipher the text. He was certain that he knew the hand, a courier who serviced Northamptonshire.

"Sir!"

He was interrupted. It was one of their clerks.

"You should see this."

"More from the pigeon loft, Sam?"

"No, sir. This is open post." *So not in code*, thought Isaiah as the clerk passed him a letter. Isaiah read silently;

Sir George Chennery has left Heathcote House. He tells me that the King's men will be seizing Colchester. He is going there.

Isaiah looked up and asked, "Whose signature is this, Sam?"

"I rather think, sir, that it is from the Duke of Northampton."

"Who is this Sir George Chennery?"

"He was on Prince Rupert's staff, sir. I think that Colonel Brydon has a particular interest in him."

"Ah. He's not one of ours, anyway. And Colchester?" he looked at Sam with an eyebrow raised. The clerk said, "Eastern Association territory." He was pointing out what Isaiah already knew — that the city was in the county of Essex, solid in its support for the Parliament.

"We'll make sure the Colonel sees this immediately he returns."

"Indeed, sir."

Isaiah turned back to his deciphering of the coded message. He wasn't — even now — particularly quick at this, and it took him the best part of an hour, but when he had completed his task, he sat for a moment thinking, his hand in front of his mouth, looking at the words he had written. Then, he picked up the papers, took up the Duke's letter from Brydon's desk, found his hat, and went immediately out to find his colonel.

By the Incarnation of Christ, he thought, and smiled at his own subconscious imitation of Oliver's words. *By the Incarnation of Christ, Great God, grant that I find the General in health. For we have need of him.*

The coded message, from an intelligencer posted in Kent — peaceable Kent, which had so far been spared any fighting in this unhappy war — gave notice that Royalists were gathering in Maidstone, the county town. *Great Lord of Hosts! Pembroke! Maidstone! Colchester! Where else?*

Not even Oliver Cromwell could be in more places than one.

*

"No father, they can accomplish all without me."

"This does not seem to me to be the same case as... before."

Josiah threw down the letter that they had been discussing. "No, it is *not* the same at all."

It was May 1648, and the hawthorn was white with flower. The land was blossoming, and the warmth of spring impregnated the farm with rich promise. They had remarked only last night upon the smell of the earth. Perhaps, this year, the harvest would be good.

The letter had informed them that the Scots had invaded England. It told them also that Royalist loyalists had seized the fortresses in Berwick and in Carlisle. And in Pontefract.

"God rot that man. More blood!" Josiah spoke with vehemence and real hate; he was referring to King Charles. He said, "Father, the reason that it is different this time is that this affair will be over soon. In weeks. I have some knowledge of our army. Believe me, he may have been taken by surprise — I had heard he had been ill — but, once he is in the saddle, Oliver will break them. Oliver and Tom Fairfax. Even if I were to go, before I've got the other side of Ipswich, news will come that this futile affair has been snuffed out. Besides, I have the farm to think of."

John smiled. Six years ago, the welfare of the farm had not deterred Josiah from riding off. *But,* thought John, *he is six years older now, and,* a sigh at the realisation, *so am I.*

Josiah, while his thinking might have been broadly correct, was premature in his declaration of the timetable. Further news came that Kent, untouched to date by war, had seen a fight at Maidstone. This matter would go forward, clearly, into further sorrow and hurt.

And then came the news from Colchester. Seized and held for King Charles, by still-loyal royalists. Colchester! Essex! There, within the hitherto staunchly Parliamentarian eastern counties. At Monks Soham they began to look at each other uneasily. Colchester was not their county town, but it was near. Too near.

*

The intelligencers of Colonel Brydon's "business" continued to feed the army's commanders a picture of piecemeal, and thankfully uncoordinated, flutters of Royalist intrigue. But by now, the real threats had become clear.

English Royalists had chosen to stir, and significant challenges were anticipated in Wales and at Colchester. Parliament's Lord-General, Thomas Fairfax, began the process of distributing his resources against the threats, ordering units into new positions. As ever, he had too few troops upon whom he could rely. The big guns were never where he needed them.

"It is all so unnecessary," Brydon complained. "Has our Lord God not shown us so many times his purpose for this Kingdom? Who are these malignants who disturb our peace, and seek to overturn His holy purposes? What is achieved, but the deaths of honest men? *Honest* men."

Isaiah Yates began to chafe at his situation, tied as he was to a job that, while it had proved initially fascinating, was not going to move him around in the way that many of his erstwhile colleagues in Cromwell's cavalry were now being ordered about. But, if he thought a staff job was going to be an idle dawdle, Elias Brydon had other ideas.

He had seen The Duke of Northampton's note. He was looking at it again when Isaiah answered his summons one late spring evening. Brydon looked up at he came into the room.

"I need you to do something. I want this man, Chennery. Sir George Chennery. His home is Heathcote House in Northamptonshire, but clearly he ain't there now. He's some kind of intelligencer for the King. In the last fight, he was a boon companion of Rupert, and, in the end, wherever he was, that became the centre of the King's effort. I have this

46

notion that George Chennery is again where their main effort lies. If he has, as we think, gone to Colchester, then that is their main thrust. Blunt it there and we break it. But *is* he there? Why should he tell the Duke? Did he think His Grace was likely to keep that destination secret? Was it bravado? Is he challenging us? I do not know. But here is what we will do. Go, and take a couple of men, and get on his trail. Start at Heathcote House. If you can, bring him in to me. If you cannot, then bring me instead news that he has died. You understand?

"Oh, and Isaiah... The Lieutenant-General wants you to have this." He passed a paper to Isaiah. It was a commission as a lieutenant-captain. "You have had the shortest period as a Cornet since Pontius Pilate. Congratulations."

5. Pembroke

Noah was rather resentful of the order. They were moving out.

He had come to like Bristol. His quarters were congenial, a warm loft above the stables of an inn. Within the same Inn, Colonel Musgrave had his headquarters.

When the moment came, Sergeant Hollin had not needed to roust out Noah's file, for the drum beating the order to fall in was very audible in that loft, the drummer performing not twenty paces away, in the street outside the Inn.

They went out of Bristol, again with colours flying, drums and fifes, then up the east bank of the Severn, seeking the bridge into Wales at Gloucester. The drums were kept working hard to make their pace. Noah said, "We are moving this time." They would do at least their twenty-five miles today.

Which proved to be so, for they were over the Severn during the morning of the second day. There, another regiment joined them to their rear. "It is Bright's regiment," Sergeant Hollin informed them. "A good regiment... well, as good as country yokels can be. Not like us Londoners, but they'll serve."

On the fourth day, approaching Raglan, four troops of horse joined them, and a company of dragoons. There was no further call for files to go out on point. From the arrival of the cavalry soldiers, they all moved within a screen of horsed men. The pace did not slacken. There was an urgency to the way they were being moved, a purpose that communicated itself from the officers to their men without spoken word.

When they sat that night around a rather weak fire they felt very privileged that their Captain came to sit with them. They were on high ground, and all around them the land fell away in wild forest. There was a wind that promised rain upon the morrow. During the day they had descended steep defiles, crossed swift streams and climbed again. The road was not much more than a track. Socks hung upon sticks over the fire, and their dinner had been biscuit.

Captain Parker was also a London man. He wore a dirty and worn buff-coat, for he had first seen service with the London Trained Bands, London's militia, and had been active defending the capital since 'forty-two. He wore also the great orange scarf and polished gorget of his office. He too looked exhausted. He had bought with him a small bottle of some spirit, which he passed around amongst the little group as they toasted their bare feet. He said, "Well, my fellow travellers, as you will know we are in Wales. We are going to a place called Pembroke. That is as far west as you can go — almost. So, a bit more travelling yet. And, I think, when we get there, we will find some malignants. I do not know much about them. But Pembroke is important. It has a castle. It is a port. It is a gateway therefore, to and from Ireland. We are going to shut the gate. You would not want King Charles up to his tricks again, and our task is to stop him from starting to do so. At Pembroke, anyway.

"We are in the hands of the Lord of Hosts. Remember that. He has shown His mighty will through the victories given to this army, of which you are now a part. A great part, for we are Musgrave's regiment, the best!" He smiled at them. "So keep yourselves amongst the saints. Pray for purity of motive. Pray for your officers. That we may have wisdom. Give God the glory."

He rose to go, but then turned back to them. "Colonel Musgrave also wants you to understand... we must consider ourselves now to be in enemy territory. We do not know what the local people will do, but we think they are sympathetic to the old church. Be on your guard. But remember, they will not speak to you in English. Just because you are shouted at, that does not require an armed response."

He had moved on to another group then with, they all thought, a similar message. Noah and his companions exchanged meaningful looks, conveying something Noah could not fully comprehend. They sat on in silence, each man absorbed in thought.

Then Noah prayed, speaking aloud. "Great God, give us this night rest and repose in your care. Drive away the ghost of fear." He remembered Captain Parker's words, and added, "We pray for our officers, that in your mercy You will give them wisdom. Amen. To you be all the glory. Amen." He felt his socks, found them dried, pulled them on, rose, shook out his blanket rolled it around him, and lay down. They were soon all asleep.

Pembroke, when they arrived outside it, was a bustle of activity. Lieutenant-General Oliver Cromwell had assembled a veritable army to effect the subjection of the town to the Parliament. Resistance to that centred upon the castle, an immensely powerful mediaeval citadel, which dominated the riverbank and port.

There had been no interdiction of the march of any of the Parliament's forces into south Wales, an indication of the weakness of their foes. But, by sheltering behind those formidable castle walls, the men ranged against them hoped that, by holding here substantial forces, others out for King Charles elsewhere might have time to inflict some stroke to restore his fortunes. Cromwell intended to deny them that opportunity.

Faced with the strong masonry, Oliver knew that he must have artillery to break it down. The question was how to bring great siege guns all across Wales, down the roads which were little more than tracks, as Noah knew. The resourceful Lieutenant-General had hit upon the idea — he would say that God gave it — to bring the guns by ship.

Musgrave's regiment arrived on the day that the great guns began to fire. It was 4 July 1648.

*

Noah and his friends had settled down to a siege. The regiment's tents were pitched in neat lines, and turn and turn about, the men were deployed into the work of digging forts, supervised by some enthusiastic, but young, officers, eager to prove themselves in this matter. Occasionally, some activity was seen atop the castle or town walls as they were observed by their enemy, but he made no effort to annoy or hinder their work.

The great guns banged and crashed. Noah wandered over once to have a look at them. Hezekiah, Moses and Mark went with him. "Now don't get in the way," said a big sergeant in a tawny coat, herding them away with his halberd. "And make sure you have no match burning. And don't light any bloody pipes."

"Hey!" said Hezekiah to his companions, "Look at that. It's a flint lock." He pointed to the firearm carried by the Sergeant's companion. "Sergeant, can we look? We have match locks ourselves."

"We are on duty, but go and ask one of the idlers over there to show you one," said the sergeant. There were tawny coated men lying together upon the grass, and Noah approached one. "Say mister, we are from

Nathaniel Musgrave's regiment. We have matchlocks, but can we look at your firelock? Only look at it. We are curious, you see."

The man gave them the sort of look that mixed pity with common experience, and held his gun out for inspection. "Its fire comes from flint against steel. D'ye see? I'll snap the lock." He pointed the muzzle safely up. "It's not loaded." He pulled the lock back with his hand so that they could see the action. The locks of their own muskets supported a match, which they had to keep burning hot, and their locks brought the burning match into the powder in the pan. But this gun was something new, pulling the trigger brought a flint to chip against a steel, sending a shower of sparks.

Noah was impressed. The man said, "you need to keep the flint sharp, but it's good."

Noah remembered flint and steel fire lighting, particularly in damp weather. "Does it never let you down?"

"Occasionally," said the soldier, "but we've always got this, ain't we?" He tapped his sword hanging at his belt. "A flintlock's no more reliable than your matches. In the wet it may be better." That was a problem; in real rain the matches, Noah knew, absorbed the damp and went out. "Anyway, we are always with the guns. And the powder. Can't have your matches burning here. There's only one match allowed by a gun, and that is guarded well. It's all the powder, see..." and he gestured at the barrels piled up in a far corner.

Yes, indeed, the burning power of exploding gunpowder had been vigorously explained to them by Sergeant Hollin. "Back in 'forty-two," the sergeant had once reminisced, "at Edgehill, at the start, I see'd a feller — absent-minded git — go to a barrel with his match burning. The good God would have had a puzzle putting him back together again. He and others. Terrible. Terrible."

The man had finished showing off his gun. "Anyway, it's called a fusil," he closed. That was how Noah found out that the tawny coated soldiers were the fusiliers, a detachment whose duty it was to guard the guns.

"It looked good, that gun," he said to Hezekiah.

"Nah!" was the response. "Too much arse-ache. Having to adjust that flint. The match is better. It'll never replace the match."

So, they gave the big cannon their full attention. There were six of them, manned by burly figures in shirts and breeches, seamen. The huge weapons were six feet long, and their muzzles looked to Noah to be ten or twelve inches wide. They watched the seamen place powder, wadding and great iron balls into them, and stood by in wonder as the fearsome things belched fire and smoke on firing. The trajectory of the projectiles could be discerned against the sky. They saw the impact upon Pembroke Castle, a cloud of dust and the suggestion of shattering of stone, and then a *whump* as the noise came back to them after a few seconds.

"I am glad they are not firing at me," said Mark Golightly.

"Amen to that,' said Noah.

There was a pause while they watched another firing. "Who is that then?" asked Noah. A man had ridden up in buff coat and feathered hat, with the familiar orange sash and gorget. He went towards the officers directing the firing of the guns. They uncovered, removing their hats in salute. He was a big framed man, heavy in his body but an agile horseman. They talked together animatedly, the man surveying the castle through a perspective glass. Noah noticed that the tawny coated sergeant was standing still and looking too.

Hezekiah held Noah's arm. "That's the Lieutenant-General. That's Old Noll. Old Ironsides. That's Oliver Cromwell." A note of awe had crept into Hezekiah's manner.

There was another huge explosion as the seamen continued their work. The *whoosh* of the cannon ball held their attention momentarily, then the *wumph* as it hit its target. Noah saw Oliver Cromwell turn his horse and trot it off.

One week later, one of Pembroke Castle's walls had crumpled to a ruin, and with a frantic beating of drums, the Royalist commanders, thinking that they had done all that honour required, surrendered the place.

The Royalist Commander, Colonel Poyer, was sent off to London, together with his three principal lieutenants, under an escort drawn from a regiment of horse. There was speculation as to their fate, because these men had previously all been soldiers for the Parliament, and were consequently seen as traitors to the cause, having been declared such by the Parliament. Seventeen others came before a local Court Martial where their peers, including Nathaniel Musgrave, sentenced them to exile, specifying that if they were caught in England after a certain date, they would be shot. It was fortunate, perhaps, for them that no Parliamentary casualty had been required to conquer Pembroke, and the victors therefore felt merciful.

The rank and file that had followed these misguided officers were deprived of their arms — including their swords — and told to go home and behave themselves better in future.

Oliver Cromwell did not wait for these footnotes to the affair. He was already racing north with his horsemen, to join General Lambert in Lancashire.

Within two days, Nathaniel Musgrave had assembled his Regiment, and colours flying and drums beating, they marched out of the Parliamentary camp at Pembroke, going first east, then north-east, following Oliver Cromwell.

6. Preston

For Noah and his companions, there was more marching then. Hard marching. Hour upon hour, tramp, tramp, tramp: left, left, left right, left. They were doing it in a state of fatigue, their bodies implementing the rhythm automatically. They no longer talked to each other, because it had all been said; every joke had been made more than once, their brains now were numbed. Noah said afterwards that he believed he was actually asleep as he went along.

It rained intermittently. Their powder, they knew, was dry within the oiled wooden flasks of their bandoliers, or tightly sealed in barrels in the wagons that went with them; their matches they kept next to the skin inside their shirts. The locks of their muskets they wrapped in oily cloth and the muzzles were likewise made watertight. Only hot action would tell if these precautions had been effective.

Noah was a small man, and light upon his feet. His shoes were standing up to the wear, but others were beginning to point to holes. And their woollen hose were becoming thin, and then toes and heels poked through, producing blisters and sore feet.

They marched north through England's midlands, through Worcestershire and into Leicestershire. They passed through towns and villages where the population withdrew into its houses to let them pass through in silence, and others where it came out to cheer them on. In one or two there were hostile looks, two fingered salutes, and the odd call of "God save King Charles." This last rather cheered them, raising a smile at its futility. Every man in the marching column knew that God had plans that would not advance the interests of King Charles.

As they wearily fell out at the end of each day of walking, Captain Parker was amongst them with encouraging words, and a report of progress. So they knew that they were part of an army concentrating to bring ruin upon the Scots.

"I am glad it is the Scots we are to fight, and not now brother Englishmen," said Mark Golightly.

"Amen to that," replied Noah. They all smiled. Mark's inability to conceal his lack of courage was, they knew, a weakness. Perhaps a potential weakness in the whole team. But he and they all knew that they would get Mark through any crisis.

Then, next day, they marched on.

Some amongst them, Paul Hollin for example, had memories of the Scots as allies at Marston Moor. These had faded by now. The religious mind of Parliament's field army was hot for the settlement of the kingdom on lines quite other than the Presbyterianism espoused by Scotland. A Scots victory would see the triumph of Presbyterian structures, a national church with national policing of belief, and an hierarchy of ministers. In Scotland that was their way. The quarrel of the Parliament's soldiers with the Scots was therefore something more than just throwing the foreign invader out of England. There was more to it than that.

At Nottingham, two wagons awaited them. These were full of new socks and shoes. There was genuine delight at the gift, and loud praise for Nathaniel Musgrave and his commissariat agents. "Oh look, just look at those," said Moses Marsh sitting down and looking in wonder at his feet in their new shoes. "Northampton leather! Praise be for the cobblers of Northampton."

Ahead, to the north, the weather looked appalling, but here the sun began to shine. They were marching again.

"How are those shoes?" Noah asked Moses Marsh, sensing an issue.

"Bloody new and stiff. I greased 'em well, but — Oh fuck it! Anyway, they rub in new places, not where the holes were..."

They were still going north. Hour upon hour they walked on. Left, left, left right, left. They did not sing now, Noah realised. They were too fatigued, and something told them to direct all their energies to their feet. So, on they went. Day upon day, with exhausted sleep at its end.

At Doncaster, someone said, "Bloody Yorkshire, in't it?"

"Aye. Black Tom's own county."

Black Tom was Sir Thomas Fairfax, the Lord General of Parliament's army, and the man of whom Oliver Cromwell was the Lieutenant.

"'e's not 'ere, is he?"

"I dunno... How would I know?" Fairfax was a talisman of success.

"Yorkshire! On to Scotland!" said Sergeant Hollin. A few smiles. They trudged on.

*

The marching column that was Nathaniel Musgrave's regiment of foot was on the road towards Skipton, having turned east and begun to climb. They were beginning to cross the hills that separate Yorkshire from Lancashire, the east from the west of northern England, the Pennines. The countryside began to get wild, remote. Noah had not seen before these bleak crags and high moorlands. It thrilled him and gave new energy to his body.

The country did not appear to have any human inhabitants. But they saw an eagle. *It is Saint John, come to have a look at us*, was the thought that struck Noah, but he did not give it voice. It was a recollection of Monks Soham, where, still chiselled in stone at the corners of the church tower were the symbols of the four Evangelists. He remembered Endsleigh Seaton explaining to him that they were the old symbols of the four gospels, a man, a lion, a something... and an eagle: Matthew, Mark, Luke and John. What was Luke's symbol? He could not recall. Yes! An ox! Meanwhile he marched on.

The road rose higher, and they passed into a mist that hid the horizon and the heights. A weak sun gave up its attempt to light their world and they passed into a damp, grey cloud. Left, left, left right, left.

And then it began to rain. Not a damp intermittent drizzle, but a continuous fall of heavy rain. There was a momentary fumbling to check that match was stowed, that rags enclosed the locks of the guns, and then a dogged acceptance of the situation. Noah dropped his head to look down, letting his hat brim protect his face from the worst of it, studying the legs and heels of the man in front. The ascent of the road was painless he realised, his physical state was so good that he was climbing with the best of them, despite the musket's weight and his knapsack.

At the close of that day, Noah and the others slept, oblivious to their soaked clothes. In the dark hours, Noah was awakened by a long, high yell. He sat up, momentarily terrified. All was quiet. Then it came again. A scream, a howling. Mark sat up too, and in the darkness, Noah could see his eyes wide and staring.

"What is that?" he asked in fright.

The howl came again. "It's Satan. Satan prowling. Holy God." Mark was shaking with fear.

"Bollocks." It was the voice of Hezekiah. "Have you never heard a fox call before? It is the young cub calling."

"We heard them in Wales too," added Hezekiah. "Did you not hear them then? Now shut up."

Noah accepted this explanation with equanimity, although he had never before heard such a call, intense and louder than anything in his experience. *A monster of a fox*, he thought but he went back to sleep.

They had two nights out in the wilderness of the Pennines, each of them punctuated by foxes howling. In the end, even Mark came to laugh at it, though somewhat nervously. "Here doggie, doggie," Hezekiah joked.

They were grateful that they were not, on those nights, required for sentry duty. Those who were, rising from an exhausted sleep to take their duty, were reminded of the need to remain vigilant despite their fatigue. Captain Parker was assiduous, when his turn of duty came, to make his visits to the sentries frequent. For a sentinel to fall asleep while guarding the camp was a court martial offence carrying a possible capital sentence. *That happens to no one, not on my watch*, thought Samuel Parker, and he turned himself out to check them, carrying his bottle of fiery spirit.

"In Christ's name, Captain, that's hot stuff," said one wet and appreciative sentinel after taking a draft, "what is it?"

"Just distilled steam from the boiling of grain," said his Captain. My father has made a fortune from the stuff." He laughed. "It'll keep you warm."

"Good man, that," said the sentry to his companion, watching the Captain's retreating figure.

Then next morning, they were off again. The rain continued. The road stretched on. Left, left, left right, left. The weak sun lifted a corner of the mist, and for a moment Noah was able to glimpse again the wonderfully bleak hillsides that surrounded them, the boulders and the heather.

He noticed also that they were no longer climbing, and they all understood this a moment later as they crossed the watershed. The mist began to lift and the road ahead sloped downward. A stream started to run alongside them on their left side and they crossed brooks that fed into it. After another hour the stream was a swift moving body of water, flowing faster than they were moving westward. The light began to sparkle upon its surface, and then their hearts lifted as the rain stopped, the mist began to disperse, and the sun began to shine.

"Praise the Lord!" said Noah. "Alleluia!"

"Amen," said several voices.

"A Psalm, I think," said Noah. And he began to sing. *Let God arise and let His enemies be scattered.* To his pleasure, the men around him joined in, the lifting of their spirits palpable. Their tired feet picked up. Up ahead, Nathaniel Musgrave looked at his lieutenant-colonel, and smiled. Left, left. Left right, left.

At last they were halted before the day had passed, and they realised that the objective towards which they had raced, had been reached.

They stood on high and open ground, from which they could look down towards a town. Their road went straight towards it. The stream upon their left had by now developed itself into a river, which sparkled in the sunshine, and, they could see, snaked past the town. Another road ran through the town, across their front, and to the left of the town it crossed the river by a bridge.

The drums beat to bring the sergeants to take their orders from Colonel Musgrave, after which Paul Hollin came towards them.

"What place is that, Sergeant?" said Noah, pointing at the town. His sergeant ignored him, and busied himself instead in detailing off watering parties and telling them they were in the likely proximity of Scots scouts.

Noah was still observing their surroundings. He had calculated that the road ran north–south, so that presumably they would turn right onto it towards Scotland.

Then Sergeant Hollin was near, and turning to Noah he said, "That is Preston. The river is the Ribble." Noah was none the wiser. All he knew was that he was a very long way from Monks Soham. He was now watching Colonel Musgrave and his staff ride down to join a group of Officers in plumed hats, and he thought the journey suggested, somehow, the promise of danger. A shiver went across his back.

They were so tired that, grateful picquet duty was not theirs, they were all asleep before dark.

*

The hammer of the drums beating to assemble them crashed out at dawn the following day. Noah and the whole file turned out as required to find the sun a pale disc still low in the sky, making for a thoroughly depressing start.

"A good day to go to glory," said Noah cheerfully to his companions. They were all nervously contemplating the probability that the Scots would have plans for them. But then Oliver Cromwell no doubt had plans for the Scots, and this thought had comforted their sleeping hours, although they had been so tired that no one had had a sleepless night, not even Mark Golightly.

The solid and reassuring figure of Paul Hollin was standing, to show where the file leader's rank was to find its right hand marker. The regiment assembled in seconds. Their first task was to draw powder again, discarding on to the wet ground what had been carried during their recent march. At the same time, new match was issued. Back in their ranks, they walked through firing by files, firing off their muskets to clear the damp. That done, locks and muzzles were wrapped again, because there was the promise of more rain.

"Good match this, it's staying hot." Noah blew upon his, keeping it burning. Then he adjusted it, and held it, as he was trained to do, between the fingers of his left hand.

As they stood in their ranks, and the sun lifted the lingering mist, their position was revealed to them. Preston was before them, at the foot of the incline on which they stood. They could see the road that crossed their front, from north to south, and as the light grew they came to see that it was full of movement, a seething grey crowd of people, horses, wagons, and here a flag, there a bright flash of colour. The Scots!

As they watched, the movement seemed still to be passing across their front, marching from right to left. From the road, there did not appear to be any deployment to face them. The town of Preston hid from them some of the Scots, and many might of course be concealed there. Between Noah's position and the houses was ground enclosed with hedges. Closer to Noah, well to the east of the road, and out of touch with it, was a body of troops. Noah counted six Ensigns. These men seemed brighter in colour, regimentally uniformed in blue, green, maroon. Whoever they were, they possessed the hedged ground, obviously deploying to use the hedges in a defence. Straight ahead, Noah judged, Musgrave's regiment had perhaps half a mile to cross before the first hedge. To his left the lane across which Cromwell had deployed his men, drove straight into the town.

Noah could see, too, lines of men, seemingly endless lines to his left and right, all in the red coats of Parliament's army. Over his shoulder he could see the second, supporting line. Immediately to their rear the red coats had bright green facings. "Hey! It's Bright's behind. They are here." There was a feeling of warmth at seeing again the "loons" of Colonel Thomas Bright's regiment, but a feeling also that they — Musgrave's — had the post of honour, in front, and that they would show Bright's how the thing was done.

Mark Golightly looked as if he would have trouble showing anybody anything. He had vomited his breakfast porridge five minutes before. But he was there in his post behind Noah, his face pale but set firmly. Hezekiah Sedgewick stood to their front, solid, immoveable. Noah was not aware of his fear, only that his guts were doing strange things.

The regiment to their right began to sing. The singing swelled and voices responded closer, so that their own ranks and files gave voice. They summoned the whole world to acknowledge the power and the glory of God. *All people that on earth do dwell, sing to the Lord,* they all sang, *Sing to the Lord.* When they had gone through it once, all started it again. It brought recollection to their minds of happier times, when with families and neighbours around them, each of them had sung these words in their home churches. It created a fierce resolution to impose themselves upon the oat-eating clowns in front of them who had once again plunged them into horrid war, who had come against them in defiance of the clear judgements of God, and in the name of that Man of Blood, Charles Stuart. Their fierce resolution was kindled into a determination that this thing was to be finished, today, when they would scatter and destroy these impudent Scotsmen. There was a collective squaring of their shoulders as each man settled to his work within a collective resolve.

Captain Parker was amongst them then, smiling at each man and saying a word there, tapping a shoulder there. He stood by Noah and looked at Mark.

Noah said lightly, "What day is this, sir?"

"It is a Tuesday, mister. It is the seventeenth day of August in this year of Grace, sixteen hundred and forty eight. It is a good day to be about the Lord's work."

"Amen. God be with us, sir."

"He is, Noah. He is. No man must doubt that. Not now, not after so many victories, so many signs of His grace." Noah was touched. His officer had remembered his name. He remembered Hezekiah's words on that march to Bristol all those weeks ago. Well, he had come many miles since then. Then he thought of Josiah Souter. Yes, he had indeed seen a little more of the world.

The drums beat and they began to advance; slowly, keeping their precise stations in their ranks and files. Paul Hollin was moving besides them. "Watch that dressing!" and "Silence!" They were moving towards the hedges. After several slow minutes of striding forward the drums halted them again, the front rank just over one hundred paces from what appeared to Noah to be a thick hawthorn barrier.

Above the drumbeat, Noah could hear another drumming; of horses. Glancing over his right shoulder, he saw horsemen coming up from the rear out beyond the regiments to his right, guarding their flank. Then Sergeant Hollin was hollering at them again. He and Captain Parker were to their front and right. The instruction came through, not wholly audible to Noah, "Folorn..." shouted Paul Hollin, pointing at the right hand file leader and with his hand signalling him and his file forward. The outer right hand file moved forward alone. When level with their Sergeant they peeled away to the left to form a new rank several paces in advance of the Regiment. "Present," came the order, then "Give fire!"

And the opening shots of what became the Battle of Preston, crashed out.

Having fired, the forward file retreated round the rear of the body, reappearing to be now the most left hand file, the men loading their muskets as they walked. Their place, exposed, out to the front was taken by the new right-most file, and so on through the musket division. A galling fire was being delivered.

When it was their turn, as Noah walked forward behind Hezekiah, Paul Hollin said "At the hedge my boys. Them's malignants behind it." And Noah made sure that he sent a ball smack into the hawthorn.

"Nicely done."

The idea that the smoothbore musket was a slow and decidedly ineffective weapon is nonsense. In the hands of well-trained soldiers, at the range at which it was used, it delivered bone shattering, body bursting damage that killed and maimed those unlucky enough to receive it. At Preston, Oliver Cromwell deployed against their foes what was probably at that time the most effective and well-trained soldiery in Europe. The men behind that first hedge, at which Noah and his companions fired, perhaps feeling themselves invisible amongst the hawthorn, found it ripped apart by the zipping of lead spheres travelling faster than light. These killed them. Those it spared took one look at their dead, and fled.

The drums of Musgrave's regiment beat again. The musket files resolved themselves again into their ranks, and each man by now with his gun held muzzle raised, but charged and ready, began to move forward. After a few moments the hedge was reached. Only then did Noah appreciate the potential problem they were up against, for the hedge prevented the regiment from advancing further. But gaps in it were quickly identified, and officers and drummers thrust themselves through. Once on the other side, the drums beat assembly frantically. Noah and the regiment flung themselves at the hawthorn barrier. Swords came out to chop the hawthorn — in spite of that half-recalled warning from Nathaniel Musgrave. The regiment burst through at several points and ran to form up on their Sergeants and Officers on the far side.

"By the Lord, but that was a close thing," said Noah. Indeed, for their foes had missed an opportunity.

Then Noah saw them. A line of men faced them across a field. The ground was close cropped, by sheep or cattle. Their foes looked to be a pike block, but there were musketeers on their flanks.

There was a buzz in the air, a whistle, and Noah suddenly awoke to the hideous realisation that he too was under fire. But the shooting was high, the balls were passing over their heads. Then Musgrave's regiment began to fire by ranks, great crashing volleys from the entire front of the musket division. Noah took his place in the second discharge, then peeled off to the rear, reloading his piece — his musket — as he went. Great clouds of smoke were left behind, obscuring the view, and soon their foes were hidden.

Judging his moment by who knows what — perhaps his soldier's instinct — Nathaniel Musgrave had his men go forward again. The regiment had two of its original six ranks still awaiting the delivery of the volley, and after an advance of perhaps twenty-five strides Noah, who had lost count, but who was now in the fourth rank, peered forward. Still he could see only thick smoke. But Nathaniel Musgrave knew what he was about. He halted his regiment, and the front rank dropped to its knee, the second rank "closed up" — their front knee touching the back of the man in front. "Give fire!" and a two rank volley rang out. Then there was a drumming of the quick march... "Club y'r muskets!" shouted Sergeant Hollin. They went forward quickly, the muskets held butt upwards to smash down their foe, the pikemen to their left advancing with their pikes held horizontal. But there was no contact. They found themselves walking over the bodies of their enemy. Where that enemy had once stood, there was at every step a body upon the ground to be negotiated. Noah knew the drill, to keep an eye out for the back of the man in front, for a fallen foe was not always out of action. But these were. They lay in grotesque postures, ashen faced, dark stains appearing on their clothing. Some quivered or thrashed in an agony, and some of these received dreadful smashes from musket butts or sword thrusts. Musgrave's regiment had found out before that mercy was sometimes repaid by their "victims" arising to kill or wound. "Better them than one of our own", was the cruel imperative.

Then they were beyond the line upon which their enemy had stood. The drums beat again and they stood, and busied themselves in dressing their ranks. "Make ready!" was again the word and Musgrave's steadied itself, preparing to renew the fight. Noah was now in the front.

There were more advances, more firing by rank, more volleys from the front two. Noah fired, and walked to the rear. He shuffled up to the front once more. He fired again. He peeled away to the rear. He reloaded. Again, and again. As he did so, he went through the nine postures of preparing his musket to deal in death, and he did not falter in this. He methodically implemented the lessons he had been taught.

They went forward yard by yard, pace by pace. Noah must have walked miles, for after each firing, he strode off to the rear of the body. They all did. Nonetheless their method and their competence ensured that they consistently made progress. An inexorable progress, relieved only by halts when they restocked their powder and bullets, of which there seemed an inexhaustible supply.

Any large view of what they were about was denied to Noah, who could see little. He was, throughout the affair, enclosed in that inpenetrable cloud of thick smoke. He was aware that there must be foe in front, but it was being exterminated by the musketry, and he was meeting only the sprawled bodies of the dead and injured. There were several hedges, in which their shot ripped great gaps, and some ditches. These last momentarily interrupted their steady progress, but they flowed across them purposefully.

The killing seemed one-sided. Hezekiah remained in the rank in front of Noah, Mark was behind. Perhaps Musgrave's was taking casualties, but Noah was not conscious that any of the people around him were hurt.

Then suddenly, there was no more firing and to their front were buildings, the town of Preston. They halted. The smoke began to clear. To their left, on up that lane into Preston, Oliver Cromwell unleashed a pursuit of a now broken and retreating foe. Above the troops to his left, Noah saw the ripple of the helmeted heads as Oliver's cavalry moved at speed into the town.

And then it started to rain. It fell in torrents. *It is as if God will wash away all that blood*, thought Noah. He tried desperately to cover his lock and the muzzle of his still-hot musket. He spent a frantic few minutes, extinguishing his match and putting it beneath his hat, realising that it was still too hot and snatching it out again, by which time it was damp. The rain was sheeting down.

Noah looked around at Mark. Mark's face was filthy, begrimed with the product of his musketry's numerous black powder explosions. Noah looked to see that Mark's coat was similarly almost black. The rain was starting to soak them. He looked at his own hands and saw they were sooty, and then he realised he too was filthy. The rain soaked them all. It ran through the black dirt, streaking their faces.

But Mark was smiling. He said quietly to Noah, "I did not run." Noah looked at him and saw perhaps for the first time the terror that had been mastered. "No," he said, "you did your duty. We both did. Alleluia!"

The man in the next file overheard. "That was more than duty. We did for them proper. Oh aye! We did for them proper." There was blood running down his face from a cut above his eye and the rain was making his shirt pink amidst the grey-black staining.

Then Captain Parker came amongst them. "Well done, lads!" Then, probably remembering his General's words, he added, "Give thanks, give thanks to the Lord of Hosts!"

"And please, O Lord, stop this fucking rain," muttered Noah's neighbour.

If any did pray for a cessation in the downfall, their God did not hear that petition, for it poured for the rest of that day. They marched about a little as they were marshalled into a pursuit column. The drummers kept their large instruments under their cassocks, but even so the weather intruded and the drums became weakened by water.

Off they went again, and when a thin sun fought its way through the rain clouds, Noah understood that they had turned south.

Cromwell had unleashed two whole regiments of horse to push into the Scots rear as they marched away. But their own horsed soldiers turned and manfully tried to cover the back of their hurrying infantry, not now more than a beaten and dispirited rabble, famished and soaked by the rain. Disarmed by poor leadership and its divided counsels, far from home, and devastated by the realisation that they were so unwelcome, the poor foot soldiers of Scotland murmured mutiny. Why had they been brought to die here in the rain, when they had thought the English kirk would welcome the deliverance they might bring? They had been told that they would deliver England from heresy, but they had met only those devastating volleys and now the slashing swords of Cromwell's pursuing cavalry.

They surrendered in droves. The Parliamentarian soldiers found them standing or squatting in the rain, their hands held high, or huddled in groups, all calling "Quarter! Quarter!" In consequence, Cromwell's infantry, including Musgrave's, frequently shed squads to shepherd the demoralised Scots into captivity. That was how Noah finished that August day. To one side of the road, perhaps seven miles south of Preston, was a field around which there was a dry stone wall, and into this enclosure went perhaps a thousand wet, miserable men. Captain Parker and the musket division were detailed off to deal with them. "If there is any trouble, you fire into them," he was instructed. Noah and the others were deployed appropriately, while in the rain Captain Parker wondered what he should do with real trouble, when the muskets were now quite useless in the wet.

It was very helpful that a series of wagons trundled up from the south, all booty 'liberated' by those pursuing cavalrymen, and stopping one, the officer of its escort shouted at Captain Parker, "How many? Biscuit here. From Scotland. Courtesy of Oliver's first regiment. The General says, give it to the prisoners."

So, the Scots were at least fed. They appreciated that they received more sustenance from their English captors than their own generals had bothered to supply. They stayed quiet. At least that way they felt less hungry.

There was, however no diminution in the rain, and all that night it fell in abundance.

7. Loyalties

All that summer there was turmoil in Josiah's mind. No news came that the matter was over, and in his mind he imagined the struggle in which his erstwhile friends in Parliament's army were engaged, and his conscience began to smite him that perhaps he should be there with them.

By September, the harvest was finished. Again, it was not so great in volume, although adequate for his plans. As they finished bringing it in, on a fine day, from his perch high upon the hay as they thatched one of the stacks, Josiah saw a horseman go into the house yard. He thought that he could recognise the man, but chose not to leave the work to others. It was only after several further hours, and with the haystack safely proofed against the autumn rain, that Josiah returned to his house.

He found Isaiah Yates seated in the parlour with his father.

"Why Isaiah, in the yard there was no sign of your horse, and I had begun to think you must have gone away again!"

"I have persuaded him to stay a night," said his father.

Isaiah Yates had risen to his feet at Josiah's entrance. He wore his red coat, with its blue facings. Josiah raised an eyebrow, conscious that he was once Isaiah's captain.

"Come sit yourself again, Isaiah. We will have no ceremonies. I am sorry I was delayed. Have you come to persuade me to re-enlist?"

"There is no need. Oliver has dealt with the Scots. At Preston."

"You must tell me about that over dinner. What has my father told you that persuaded you to stay?"

"Ah! My orders allow one night's lodging on the way. Shall I pay you the conduct-money?"

"Pish, man! Spend it on beer. From whence have you come? And where are you bound? I hoped for your sake that you had gone home for good. But here you are, still in harness as a soldier."

"I could not stay at home, Josiah. I work on Oliver's staff, now. And I'm from Colchester. Although Oliver was not there."

"You have been at Colchester?"

"Aye. With Tom Fairfax. He broke the Kentish affair. Now he's broke the Essex lot."

"He would do that. Did he do it well?"

"Oh Yes! He did it well."

"It is over?"

"Oh Yes. It is over."

And with their dinner of roast pigeon, prepared by Phoebe, Isaiah told Josiah the story. How the resistance at Colchester had been stubborn, and a siege of six weeks had been required to subdue it. And how at the end, Fairfax had taken two Royalist leaders and had them shot.

"'Tis true. Not in hot blood, but in cold. They had given their parole you see. Earlier. The first time we captured them. In 'forty-five. Had given solemn oaths, never again to take up arms. And here they now were, caught again fighting in the same bloody cause, leading a six-week resistance for that Man of Blood. Resistance too of what we know to be the manifest will of God. O Lord, you should have seen our dead. And wounded. I'd have shot more. But all the rest, Black Tom sends home. Except..."

"*Except?*"

"Except some of our own, Josiah. This time there were men there who had served the Parliament. Now out for the king."

"How so?" Josiah was thoroughly shocked.

"Presbyterians, see. Our great King Charles, your sovereign head of the Church in England, with his bishops and crosses, priests and prayer book. When it suits him. What did he do? Told everyone now he'd establish instead the presbytery in England."

"No!" Josiah remembered Oliver's words, *enslavement by canting presbyters*. "We all thought the king repudiated the Presbytery. That he would rather to see the Mass return than Presbyterians."

"Yes, that's what our royal friends always told us when we had them corralled the first time. A big man for bishops and the Book of Common Prayer, was King Charles. But clearly that was only when it suited him."

"And now he seeks to divide us — the Parliament party. He seeks to bring the Presbyterians over to his side." Josiah saw the weight of opinion that might build up against his friends.

"Not just 'seeks'. He succeeds." Isaiah was grieved.

"But the army?"

"The army does not change, Josiah. Not where it matters. It is no more inclined to place canting Presbyterians over us than canting priests." Josiah thought he heard an echo of Cromwell in the old Ironside.

"But you said some of ours were…"

"Not where it matters. No. A few outposts and garrisons. Left over remnants from the old aristocrats' companies. The field army is with Oliver. It is a gathered church still, a company that knows God. It is wondrous. And it is still hot for toleration. Tolerance. Independence for the church, for England."

"But Parliament..."

"What is Parliament without the army?"

"Yes. What indeed. Oliver was ill… "

"Yes, and very seriously. It was that I think that kicked life into this whole late affair. They thought he was a goner, maybe. Anyway, his grip was loosened. Colonel Poyer — you remember him, pompous arsehole — he, of a sudden, decided he was holding Pembroke Castle for the King, not the Parliament. He forgot his solemn oath and all. He was the first."

John Souter, who was of course eating with the pair of them, was now genuinely puzzled. "I do hear Pembroke castle is mighty strong."

"Yes. Oliver had to get great guns there to subdue it, sir."

"But he did?"

"Oh yes. He did. Oliver does things, sir. Mighty things. Oliver does not allow God to be mocked. Oh, no! And then he was off to deal with the Scots. Who, of course, would be for Presbytery. Yes. Well, we know now what God thinks of their plan to fasten their presbytery upon England's neck. I was not there, but the talk is that Oliver allowed the Scots down through Lancashire — so he could then get behind them."

"Across their lines of communication..."

"Yes, then fell on them. Jesus, but they must have been sad. Smashed them he did, drove the remnant all the way to Warrington. Pinned them against the river — the Mersey. The great Duke o' Hamilton didn't do too well. Some of his horse ran as far as Uttoxeter, but his foot... they finished in Warrington."

"What happens to them, poor fellows?" John Souter was sad for them. He had seen his own son ride off to war.

"Some — those who volunteered — goes to a new life in the sugar islands, sir. There the presbytery can have them."

Isaiah clearly did not give much thought to Scotsmen shipped off to the West Indies. He was rushing on. "But, Josiah, the talk is now all of vengeance. After Naseby and Torrington, after the fall of Oxford, in 'forty-five to six, we were generous. Their men all sent home with conduct money. All the talk was of reconciliation, peace and accommodations with the King. Now it is different. It is *different.*"

"How so, Isaiah?"

"Now it is all talk of vengeance. Of now dealing with the chief delinquent. No more tip-toeing around his majesty!"

"There was a resolution, was there not, in Parliament — no more addresses?"

"Yes, there was. No more talking. This is more than that, Josiah. This is exemplary justice on the Man of Blood himself. They talk of..." Yates hesitated, glancing at John Souter, anxious lest he offend his old host.

Josiah pressed him, "Of what, Isaiah?"

Yates looked straight at the younger man, and said boldly, "I think they will put the King on trial for his life."

"But how... what... how could that be done?"

"By the same power that tumbled his soldiers. The power that delivered God's judgement upon the nation. The power of Naseby. By the army."

"Would it just be a murder? There are precedents for that."

"No, a public trial. We say before the whole nation just what it is that he has done. That he has bathed this nation in blood. That he has defied the judgements of God, given in the field. That he has never negotiated in good faith."

"A trial! The law gives no precedent. I know enough law to know that."

"Then we make a precedent. The King answers to us for his conduct. To the people. And, afterwards, once the precedent is there, no more arbitrary power from any King. Or anyone else. That's a precedent worth setting. Yes, indeed."

Josiah thought. *Yes. It is. Praisegod would have approved.*

*

The next morning, Isaiah Yates was off early, and Josiah was up and outside to see him go. They shook hands, and Isaiah retained his hold of Josiah, and with his left hand held his elbow, looking into his eyes.

"Captain," he said, returning to the formality they had known together in the Ironsides, "Captain, you have here a woman named Phoebe Hetherington?"

"Yes, Isaiah. It was Phoebe that cooked the dinner you enjoyed last night." Josiah was taken aback. "Why?"

"This may not happen," said Isaiah. "But she came, did she not, from Heathcote in Northamptonshire?"

"She did. But...?"

"I do not seek to disturb her. Or you. However..."

"And?"

"Her previous employer was Sir George Chennery. Josiah, you need to know that George Chennery was in Colchester."

"George... Ah!" Josiah was beginning to see where this was going.

"You know of him?" Isaiah was alert, eyeing Josiah strangely.

"I have ... heard of him. Phoebe has told me of him. And I met him once. When I brought her here." He did not tell Isaiah of Praisegod, and how they had come up against George in King's Lynn. It was old history. Past.

But Isaiah was all ears. "He was not, as far as I could ascertain amongst the dead there. At Colchester. He is not, I think, amongst the prisoners. So where is he? We do not know. Josiah, we think him to be a most dangerous malignant. Dangerous. And I am sent to fetch him in. That's why I'm riding around. On his trail. I'm bound now for Lynn. That's one place from which they get out of England, the malignant fugitives..."

"From Lynn! From Lynn? It's a Parliament town. Surely?" But Josiah knew, only too well, that it was not.

"If I find him, Isaiah went on, I'm to bring him in to Oliver, to Elias Brydon."

"Oh *him*. You work for *him*."

"Aye."

"God speed you then." Josiah stepped back and Isaiah heaved himself up into the saddle. The horse was a grey stallion. From his higher station, Isaiah looked down at his friend.

"But Josiah, if he comes here..."

"Why should he come here?"

"I don't know. To persuade Mistress Hetherington, perhaps... to help him get away. To get money from her... I don't know. But if he *does* I say, turn him in. He is a key man, Josiah. If I see him, I'll pistol him. And that'll do him a favour, because Oliver'll shoot him. But if he comes here, get word to Ipswich. There's patrols out from there, now. They'll be looking for malignant fugitives. They'll nail him. And don't let any regard Mistress Hetherington has for him, get you and Mister John into any trouble. You know, it's getting nasty — I told you last night — and sheltering these coves is dangerous... to you."

"I know my duty, Isaiah," said Josiah, and at that moment, he did.

*

Then the autumn of that unhappy year closed in around the Souter farm. The days were shorter and the evenings dark. In November, a news-sheet announced the great peace made in Germany which ended three generations of warfare there. It speculated that now, his hands free, the King of France might assist his brother monarch in England.

This news was swiftly followed by more, of the murder of Parliament's Colonel Rainsborough in his quarters in Doncaster. Perhaps that threat from France — more imagined than real — and that very real murder by desperate Royalists, hastened on the army's next move.

As he came for his dinner one evening a few days later, Josiah found John Souter reading a third news-sheet. The older man had to hold the paper close to the candles in the already dark room. Josiah lit several more to assist him.

"See here Josiah," he read, *"The Remonstrance of the Army.* This news-sheet." John read from it, "What fine words..... *We demand justice for our dead..... The sovereignty of the people.* What is that? The sovereignty of the people?"

"I like the sound of it."

"Yes. But see here. It is just as your friend Isaiah said." He read again, *"That the person of the King be speedily brought to justice for the treason...* Treason! The King! How can *he* do treason? But they mean it, Josiah, they mean it. *Treason against the People of England..."*

72

John Souter went on reading, "And how is it made lawful? *This army be a lawful power called by God to oppose and fight against the King...*Called by God.'"

"Yes," said Josiah, "So it be. So it really do be. I can hear him saying those words, father."

"Hear who?"

"Oliver. Mister great heart. Oliver Cromwell. He will act in obedience to a higher law."

Josiah went and stood looking out of the window. John could not well see the reflection of his face, but he looked at his son's back.

Thoughts of England's woes disappeared. *What my boy needs*, he thought, *is the solace of a good woman's love. That would heal all, make all, seal all.* And, he reflected, allow himself, John, to die in peace. For Josiah would make a son, or sons, and that was a matter that the older man had come perhaps overmuch to care about, to ensure that the Souter name continued, and that the farm went on in the Souter line. *Happy shall the man be, who has his quiver full,* thought the ageing squire of Monks Soham, quoting Psalm 27, in which the Hebrew poet sings of the joy of parenting.

He said, "Josiah. I have given much thought recently to the future. You should marry."

"Father! What has brought that idea forward?"

"Two things. First, I am old. I must expect to go to judgement one day not so very far away. Oh, I do not fear that: Christ's Blood has ever been my justification. But before God calls me to glory, I should like to see a third generation here. A grandson. Or a little granddaughter," his thoughts began to wander and he recalled himself sharply, "but preferably a son. And second, you are of the age when these things are done best. You are not young, inexperienced, silly. The Lord knows you have seen more than I had at your age. But another five years, and the girls will think you old. So, what do you think?"

Josiah turned into the room.

His father continued. "I have not asked. Were there women when you were away? As a soldier, did you have opportunity?"

"No. father. There were no women. We were not a debauched company. Such licence would have brought trouble. Our lives in the Ironsides were as celibate as the monks of old. Our discipline held."

"Forgive me for my direct speech. You are then inexperienced in these matters."

"As a maiden." Josiah laughed as he thought of it, but without bitterness, just at the paradox. He had fought, he had killed, but he was without sexual experience.

"Then, my dear boy, we could do worse than consider a widow."

"Which widow would meet with your approval? You have some match in mind, father. I will not wed the widow Thompson." The reference was to the widow of an Ipswich lawyer, known to them both.

"She is reputed to be monstrously wealthy, Josiah. And reportedly keen to find a new man."

"I do not doubt that she will. But not me."

"No," said John. Then making up his mind and ploughing on, "who would come into your own mind, Josiah, in this connection?"

Josiah paused only momentarily, then looked his father fully in the face. "Susanna", he said, "our Susanna."

8. Testing

Charlie had listened well to Ebenezer's lessons, not least in the matter of taking rabbits. Remembering his father, he had perhaps something of the huntsman in his blood. He would silently leave the house early in the morning, and purposively move around the area, to inspect the lures and loops that he had set the evening before. He found that when he was successful, the result was most welcome to Phoebe, who took advantage of his skill to eke out the household's food budget. Charlie was rewarded, he thought handsomely.

He loved the loneliness of these morning patrols, relishing the crisp clear newness of the rising sun scattering the mists of the dawn. On one such morning in November, he was returning with two brace of coney hanging from each of his two hands, oblivious to everything except his pleasure in such a good haul. As he came up to the house through the orchard, he was alarmed and he took real fright when he found a man lying to one side of the path, under the trees. At first he thought he might have stumbled upon a corpse, but the body moved, heaved itself to sit up against a tree, and spoke.

"Boy! Come here". Charlie saw the man was cloaked and booted, but was soaking wet. His head was uncovered and his face white, sickly and glistening with sweat. Charlie saw that he was ill or hurt, and his fright began to diminish.

"Sir?"

"You know the house — yonder."

"Aye, sir. I'm in service there."

"Are you... Do you know a Mistress Hetherington? Phoebe Hetherington?"

"Yes, sir, I do."

"You listen here." The man's tone was imperious, short. He moved, pushing with his left arm upon the ground. The cloak fell off his shoulder, and Charlie saw that he was wearing a sling, his right arm apparently held immobile. The man's face winced at the effort to move and he lay as if the effort had taken all his remaining strength. He said, "You get Phoebe here. I would talk with her."

"Sir." Charlie did not hesitate. Phoebe he knew would sort this matter out.

"And boy. No one else must know about me being here. Phoebe would want that kept a secret. Understand?"

Charlie nodded vigorously. He ran to the kitchen. He thought it likely that Phoebe would be about, as was her custom, reviving her oven fires, and he was not wrong.

"Bless you child. It looks as if you've seen a ghost." As he had known she would, she listened to his message. She gave no clue that she might know who the man was. She said merely, "he is in the orchard is he?" And she threw her shawl about her, and went out, saying, "No you stay here. Go about your business as usual Charlie."

She shut his protest, by adding, "If it is who I think it is, I am in no danger."

And later, Josiah was eating his breakfast ham, and planning the day's work. The harvest was in, but the dairy work continued, the pigsty needed rerooting, and equipment needed its maintenance and overhaul in preparation for the next year. He became aware that Phoebe was in the room, and looked at her, with a smile.

"Sir, may I speak with you?"

"Of course, Phoebe. What ails you?"

"There is a man hiding in the orchard. He is Sir George Chennery, that was my employer in Heathcote House."

Josiah felt a small twist grow inside him, an anxiety, because he knew what was coming next. He thought of Isaiah's warning.

"He was out for the king, in Colchester. He is now a fugitive, sir. And he is hurt. Quite bad, as I judge."

Josiah looked at Phoebe. He wanted to ask what he was supposed to do, but he thought Phoebe deserved better. Besides, her instinct was right to tell him, and he saw that it was to himself and his father that her loyalty now lay. She was not concealing George Chennery's presence.

"If he is hurt, Phoebe, we must look to his care."

"But sir. He is a fugitive from the Parliament's army..."

"Yes." Josiah thought, yes, the man had given his oath, broken his word, gone again to war and would be executed when he was caught. Isaiah had said as much.

Phoebe said, "Sir, this man was — is — the brother of my Lady Jane, she who Praisegod was working alongside, while he lived."

"Ah!" Yes, a telling point, Phoebe. "Will he take kindly, do you think, to being entertained by us Roundheads?"

"Sir, he looks to me in no condition to raise any objection. He seems hurt bad."

"Then we must bring him in."

And so, a party of men went with Josiah into the orchard, found the fugitive collapsed unconscious, helpless. He was taken into a guest room.

John Souter had joined them to discover what the fuss was all about.

"Ebenezer. Off you go to Ipswich. Fetch the surgeon," he said.

Josiah said, "Take Judgement. Quick as you can."

"I'll take Marigold, sir. Thank'ee. Judgement will take too much managing."

"Whichever... just go quickly man."

When he was laid on the bed, the full extent of George Chennery's condition became apparent. He had clearly been out living rough for some days. He was dirty. Worse, his face was deathly pale, white and glistening with sweat. There was a black stain over his blue coat, and recent red blood leaching through the sling at his shoulder. The women stood looking at him, until John galvanised them into action.

"Get him washed. Get him a clean shirt and get him into that bed. Come on. You have all seen a naked man before. Take all his clothes and burn them. Including those boots. Get that wound washed if you can."

"And watch him," said Josiah.

His father said, "He must rest. If he recovers his senses, tell him he is quite safe. No one will betray him, without my authority. And I choose to give him shelter."

He turned to Josiah and said, "He has run from Colchester."

"Yes."

"Will the army be looking for him?" Josiah saw Phoebe look towards him.

"They will be, yes. But we have him secure. He won't run in a shirt."

Old John said, "he is some man's son."

"He is a malignant. A servant of the Man of Blood. I will help him recover his health, because that is only charitable. But after that, I do not care if he is hanged."

"They won't hang him, Josiah. He'll lose two years' income, or perhaps a sixth of his land, but they'll not hang him."

"Maybe they should."

"Josiah, for the love God bears to you, master this harshness."

"Yes. I will. For your sake, father. And for Phoebe's." He caught her eye, remembering his friend. "And, perhaps for Praisegod's sake too."

"I thought *he* would be hot for vengeance."

Josiah looked at the broken body. "Maybe he was, but were he here now, after it is all over, I think he too might think more gently."

The surgeon did not arrive that day, and Josiah felt obliged to visit his injured guest.

George Chennery was conscious, but clearly weak and in pain. His breath came noisily, and Josiah, looking at him, thought it possible the hangman would be cheated by the injury. He looked sick to death.

To his surprise, George spoke as soon as Josiah entered.

"I thank you, sir…. For your hospitality."

"It is our Christian duty, Sir George."

"You have the advantage of me. For, you know my name, but I have no knowledge of yours."

Well, you have, thought Josiah, *for I stole your cook, and she is why you are here*. But he dissembled and introduced himself, adding, "the surgeon is on his way."

"That is more than duty Mister Souter. I thank you again." There was a pause, then, "I think it possible that you do not approve of me?"

"If you have been, as I think is so, out for the King then, no I do not approve of your action. But as for yourself, well, I do not know you, or why you have so acted, and therefore cannot presently say if you have my approval or not." Josiah heard himself speaking formally.

A smile came across George Chennery's pallid face. "I am not in a position to …"

"No, sir. You are not in a position to do other than…. this. You will rest, and await the surgeon." Josiah recalled his father's words, and found himself saying, "You can be easy. No one from this house will betray you to the army of Parliament. Not because we have sympathy with your fight, quite the reverse, but simply because to do so would be for us a betrayal of a higher duty of hospitality."

"I thank you for that."

"I am sorry for your injury, Sir George. Tell me what happened. It may help me to brief the surgeon, if — "

"If I drift off again. Yes. We were running. We turned our backs and ran. From the rebels. They shot at us from behind. I took a ball in my shoulder. I had already a wound there, but a ball hit my shoulder, and then another in my back. They must have struck my horse too, because he carried me only another four hundred yards, and then dropped dead and threw me into a ditch. Pursuit went past. I walked."

"Colchester is thirty miles off."

"Well it has taken me several days. I was heading for Heathcote. For home."

Phoebe interrupted them, by coming in. Josiah was relieved, saying, "Ah! Here is Phoebe. What's there? A soup? A treat for you, Sir George. Try to get some down you."

"Sir. Thank you." George Chennery, for one of very few times in his life, was genuinely humbled.

*

The surgeon came the following morning, and probed into the wounds of Sir George in order to extract musket or pistol balls. He inflicted unspeakable pain upon his patient, and sucked his teeth afterwards as he looked down at the wounded man, by now in complete collapse. What he had to say, as he took his fee, led Josiah to believe that George would soon be dead. "His right shoulder is shattered. There is bleeding into his lungs. The pain has imposed such a strain upon his heart... If he is alive in two days, he may recover. But I think it unlikely."

Endsleigh Seaton, the Vicar of Monks Soham, had taken it upon himself to attempt to prepare George for eternity. A Cambridge man, and a zealot for the further reformation of the Church of England, Endsleigh was nonetheless a person of real compassion. People, puritan people like the Souters, said of him that "he walked with Christ". That was to say of Endsleigh all that he wished said about himself. So, this worthy and loveable man sought to extend the love of his Saviour to the broken Cavalier. Sadly, George Chennery was in no state to respond, drifting in and out of consciousness, and irrational at best. Endsleigh was not a man to shirk his work, however, and he sat for hours at the injured man's bedside, in prayer, or reading his Bible.

"I have a vision, sir," he said to Squire Souter, who had looked in to himself assess the progress made by his guest. "I have a vision of this man praising God, and amongst His elect."

"In heaven, Endsleigh, no doubt. For to me he looks too tired to linger in this world."

"Ah. Yes. I cannot say whether 'twas this side of death or the other. You are right. He is weaker, I think."

"I do not think he will last this night."

But George Chennery did not die. He survived that night and the next. The surgeon's two days passed, and George was still breathing. Phoebe and Susana took turns to spoon boiled water into him, and thin soup. On the third day, Phoebe reported to Josiah; "I think Sir George will not die."

"Has he spoken to you?"

"No, sir. But he is... the fever is less hot."

"That is good to hear, Phoebe. Thank you. What you are doing must continue. It is working. Can you maintain it?"

"Yes, sir. I must. I owe it to Jane."

Josiah thought, *but not to him, not to George.* Then he thought that, in his heart, he himself hoped that George would in fact die. Because, if he lived, then those questions of duty and loyalty which had been deferred, would require to be resolved, and — what was worse — be acted upon. Deep in Josiah's subconscious lay an overwhelming loyalty to that cause to which he had given three years of his life. He knew that he should secure the capture of this malignant, George Chennery, and take him right out of the fight.

He began to think of the letter he would write, to bring the Parliamentary gaolers to the house.

*

If Josiah resolved that George Chennery was going to be handed over to Parliament's army, his father had other ideas.

Josiah heard his father's view over dinner.

"I rejoice that the man is not dying. Do you not?" the older man asked his son.

"I do, father." Josiah's tone belied the words.

"And what do you think his *not* dying means, Josiah? It means that the Lord has delivered him. The Lord has some further purpose for him Josiah. He has given this man more time, to repent, to act for the gospel, for who knows what? But God knows.

"He is a broken body, Josiah. He will not go off soldiering again. Not for King Charles. Not for anyone. He will not ever again be capable of wielding sword or pistol." Josiah could see that his father was adamant. He was also correct in his assessment of their guest's health.

John continued, "And there is the further point, Josiah, that he is our guest. Does the hospitality of the Souters allow you to hand a guest over to his enemy? By the very incarnation of Christ, Josiah, what would that make us be? And one further point occurs to me, my dear boy." John Souter was always at his most patronising when he was insistent. "You are still very sure that the King's party are humbled. I wish I was so sure. I think we need to consider — oh not just yet, but one day sometime — that the King's party may wax strong again. And at that moment it would suit me fine if there was one Royal partisan I had treated well, an example I could use then to avert their wrath."

Josiah knew that he was in filial duty bound by the older Souter's decision. He asked, "What would you have me do?"

"The least we do is this. When he is fit, he wanders away from here without our informing anyone. But let us do better Josiah. Let us seize the moral high ground. Let us heap coals of fire upon his malignant head. Let us send him off with twenty pounds, and our good wishes."

"Oh father. You are set upon this, are you not?"

"I am set upon not bringing the army here to take him away as their prisoner. Yes."

"I will think upon it."

"No, Josiah. I am your father. You will not think, you will do this. For me. You will not do it because you owe me obedience, I see. Do it then for the love you bear me."

Josiah had one last throw. "Father, the man is a malignant... An oath breaker. I know him to have been engaged in subversive work. He even lied about not knowing my name."

"Oh Josiah, listen to yourself. Take off your soldier's coat. It never fitted you. You said so yourself. Let compassion reign, Josiah. What would Christ expect us to do? Eh?"

Josiah sensed his defeat. He said, "This course you plot will, I think, take courage."

"For him? Or for you?"

"Well, for me, actually."

"Then," finished his father, "if that is so, I say it is the right course. For you."

Josiah then adopted his father's point of view, though he was afterwards unsure of why he did so. It was not from compassion for George Chennery. Perhaps his father's arguments had been genuinely persuasive. Perhaps he did it for Phoebe. That meant — really — he did it for Praisegod's memory.

He pushed Isaiah Yates, and his words of warning from his mind and ignored them. Then, he sent Ebenezer off on a mission.

"Go to Lynn, Ebenezer. King's Lynn. I will give you money. Go into the *Mermaid Inn*. Take a room there. Just for two nights. Find the ostler there, and a boy who works with him. Tell that lad that you want to get in touch with Simon, or Steve — Stephen maybe. When you are satisfied that you are speaking with either of those two, tell them I sent you. When they remember me — and they will — you will know you have found the right men. Say to them that I have a job for one of them. Ask one of them to come here in say, three weeks time. Give them a sovereign on account."

When Josiah had last been in Lynn, he had made the acquaintance of these two boys, and they had been invaluable to him in his endeavour to secure justice. And vengeance. It was an irony that they had — amongst their duties for him then — been required to stalk George Chennery.

George, as Phoebe had predicted, improved. John too had been right. Josiah saw that it was impossible that George would ever recover the use of his right arm, and movements gave him pain, so that he winced frequently. But he was, within a month, able to heave himself up in order to be propped upon pillows as Phoebe and Susanna continued their ministrations. And he had completely recovered his wits.

Josiah had visited his unwelcome guest each day to monitor progress, and waited, to judge his moment. The last thing to be desired was that George would anticipate matters by running away. The daily visit meant that they spoke together, but of very little that had any importance, although Josiah made sure that what news he had was passed on. This gave him some pleasure, for the news indicated that the King's cause was irretrievably lost — at least in military terms — and the final royal gamble had achieved nothing. The Presbyterian party had been tumbled alongside King Charles, and now the army was unchallenged in its supremacy. And if the army was supreme, then so was the cause of independency — the idea that there would be toleration in religion, with gathered companies of believers free to worship as they wished, unpoliced by bigoted kings, bishops or presbyters.

He said, "We should, I think, give some thought Sir George to what happens next."

"To me?"

"To you. What would you do? You said you were seeking to get to Northamptonshire. But consider, sir. Is that safe?"

"No. It is not."

"No. The army will be seeking you. They will find you. It is in my mind that you must leave the country." Josiah saw the question arise in George's face. "We will assist you, yes. We have our reasons. I am not hot for the idea, but neither can I see you taken. Not from here. I have contacts, of a sort, in Lynn. I have reminded some friends of mine who are there. They will be here in the next few days. We will talk with them, but my idea is that you go with them and they will assist you to take a ship…"

"Where to?"

"I have no idea, Sir George. Where will your friends be? The Prince of Wales? That German Prince … Rupert? Are they in Holland? In France? Go there. Will they not receive you?"

"Rupert will. I was with him … in his Lifeguard. But I must go first to Northamptonshire, to my home. I must raise money."

"No, that would prove your undoing. And possibly mine too. There will be a spy posted somewhere. Look, my father and I can send you off with ten, no, twenty pounds."

"You would do that for me?"

"We would do that for you. Yes. Once you are away with your friends, then send letters to your home, if you will. Raise money and get it to yourself. These things can be done. Some Jewish banker somewhere, perhaps?" Josiah thought of Doctor Cooper, a Jewish doctor who had befriended him.

"Sir, I would be... forever in your debt."

"Ha! Well, my father was saying... Well, no matter what my father was saying... Let us talk more of this plan. But later. For now, think on it. Think where you might go."

"Mister Souter, I am genuinely at your service, and most grateful. I do not know how to thank you."

"Let us get it done before that concerns you, sir. Let us first get it done."

Three days later — earlier than anticipated — Ebenezer was back, reporting that he had made contact with Josiah's erstwhile friends.

*

In the event, those who sought to capture George came unbidden by any letter.

And Josiah's hesitations vanished in the face of their arrogant intrusion.

Josiah was speaking with Ebenezer by the pump in the house yard, when Josiah felt — through a tremble in the ground — the not unfamiliar approach of horsemen. He reached out and held Ebenezer's arm as the older man too registered the approach. "Steady Ebenezer. Calm. Do not let our alarm put us off our guard. They will sense any unease."

Then Charlie came sprinting into the yard, "Soldiers! Soldiers coming!" He raced across to Josiah and stood behind him.

"Steady, Charlie," said Josiah.

"Quiet, Charlie," said Ebenezer. "Do not give the game away." Josiah had only time to register that Ebenezer had embraced the idea that they were not about to surrender George Chennery to the Parliamentary army, before the source of the disturbance clattered into the yard. It was six troopers of the army's horse, led by a very youthful Cornet.

The troopers, by a clearly pre-arranged plan, took themselves around the yard and stood their horses, while their young officer brought his mount over to Josiah. Ebenezer had put an arm around Charlie's shoulders. The boy was breathing heavily.

"Good day, sir," the officer began. "In the name of the Parliament of England, we are here…"

Josiah realised afterwards that he quite enjoyed the encounter. This surprised him, for in thinking about it, he realised upon reflection that he could have handled it better. But it was the sheer effrontery of this mere boy, bringing such a large horse on to his — Josiah Souter's — property and treating its owner so dismissively! He recalled his status as an old Ironside, and looked around the men who were with this youngster. He found what he hoped for, a face he knew.

"Good day sir! And John Wainwright! A good day to you. How are you? I see you are now a corporal-of-horse. Well done."

Corporal Wainwright flushed, and looked at his officer. "Good day, Captain Souter."

"My dear chap. Have a glass. Oh Cornet, forgive me. You too. Charlie, Ebenezer, my compliments to Phoebe, and small beer for these gentlemen. There are seven of them." Ebenezer and Charlie went to the house. Josiah turned back to the Cornet.

"What brings you here, sir?" He was feigning affability, delighted that it discomfited the new arrival.

"We are from the army of Parliament, sir. We are seeking fugitive malignants, the remains of King Charles' soldiers. Many are fled and infesting the country. They are a menace to peace of this nation. I am in receipt of a report that one was seen coming in the direction of your farm."

Josiah furrowed his forehead. "When was this?"

"As to that, precision escapes us, sir. Within the last few days. Since the fall of Colchester. About which you have heard, no doubt."

"Yes. I had heard. And have you found any of these men..."

"Sir, that is no concern of yours. I ask if there is any such here?"

Josiah was thoroughly resenting this young man's arrogance. He straightened his back, and said with affected asperity, "Sir, I was an officer in Oliver Cromwell's first regiment and served with him for over three years, as Corporal Wainwright there will attest. This house is known as being for the Parliament in these troubles, being strongly for the Parliament's interests, as any of my neighbours will confirm. Is it likely that a malignant would seek, and find, shelter here? No."

"Sir, he might be hiding..."

"No, Cornet. Not here. My land is walked over daily. My outbuildings are in use continually. Without exception," Josiah added.

"I would search..."

"No Cornet. You waste your time." Josiah looked the boy straight in the face. He thought of George Chennery's broken body. "And were there to be here anyone *who was a menace to the peace of this nation,* he would by now have been apprehended. And as an Ironside officer, I would know my duty to hand any such over to yourself."

Josiah was aware the beer was going around. Phoebe appeared at his elbow, holding a tray towards the boy. From his high perch, the Cornet looked at it, and Josiah thought for a minute that he would refuse it, but then the youngster curtly nodded at them both, reached down, and took the tankard.

There was a complete silence in the yard. Josiah stood looking at their officer as the soldiers drank.

Phoebe then moved, collecting empty tankards, which the troopers returned with words of thanks and the odd smile. Their officer was concluding that he was indeed searching in the wrong place, when John Souter came ambling into the yard, stiffening at the sight of armoured and mounted troopers there.

His advent made the young officer pause to review his evaluation of the position. He said to John, "You there, sir! Who are you?"

"He is not a malignant, sir!" Josiah made of it a joke. The troopers smirked.

"By the Lord, I am John Souter. And this is my property. What are you here about?"

"They seek men who are *a menace to the peace of this nation,* father," said Josiah, "and I have assured them no such are here."

There was the smallest of looks from father to son, before John said, "I should say not. Why if I found any man here that could fight for King Charles, he'd feel my own stick on his arse."

The Cornet held his tankard out to Josiah, who took it, while continuing to look coolly upon his visitor. The boy said, "Should any such arrive here, sir, you will know what to do."

"Indeed."

The young officer turned his horse and trotted out of the yard. His men followed, and Corporal Wainwright saluting Josiah as he passed, pulled a face, which seemed to suggest some discomfort with the regime under which he now served. Josiah noted sadly that the horses moved in a weary and fatigued way.

"And we told him no lies!" John Souter said to his son. "But by whose authority are they here, invading my land, threatening…"

"Hush father, hush. Let us forget it. There was no impropriety. They did not exceed their orders. As for their authority — well," Josiah recalled a pistol he had once lain before the Mayor of King's Lynn — "all their authority is in their swords and pistols."

"I think we shall see more of that sort of authority in the future," said John Souter. And he went inside the house.

9. Plots

Ebenezer's foray into Norfolk had been faultless. And precisely on the twenty-first day after the old man's return, Josiah was told, "A fellow is at the door asking to see you, sir."

On his threshold, Josiah found his friend Simon. But a Simon changed. The cheeky grin still enlivened the face, which was unmistakably his. But this was a young man now grown taller, and filled out.

"'Tis me, sir!"

"Yes. Simon. It is good to see you. Come in, come in."

They sat together. Simon explained his changed circumstances.

"I am the tapster now at *The Angel Inn*, sir. Regular job. And... and Lucy — you remember Lucy Gill, sir — she's my girl now." Josiah had never met Lucy, but she had been part of the gang that had shown itself such an effective spy network in King's Lynn. He knew Simon to be of great intelligence, if very humble birth, and he fancied Lucy would be well founded.

"That's good, Simon. Invite me to the wedding."

"I don't know about that, sir. Weddings is not for the likes of us."

"She deserves nothing less, Simon."

"So, this business you wished to discuss, sir?" Simon was changing the subject, and Josiah let him.

"Yes. What I need is this. I have an injured man upstairs. He will be fit to move very soon. This is what I need. I want him taken quietly into Lynn, and put aboard a ship. And no questions asked. As I say, all done *very quietly*."

"And taken where, sir?"

"I don't know that. Yet. Tell me first, whether what I ask can be done. Tell me of any ships you might get him onto. Quietly. Then where that ship might go — and that may be where we must send him."

"I see. This man a friend of yours, is he?"

"Not exactly."

"But he's in danger. You spoke of moving quietly."

"Let's say, I would wish to avoid Parliamentary army entanglements."

"The Parliamentary army? But you are on their side."

Josiah nodded. "But *he* was not."

"Oh, I see. He is a friend of yours? Well, obviously, he is. Silly question."

"No, Simon. It is not silly. No, he never was a friend of mine. And no, I do not want him as a friend now. But I have acquired a debt of honour. Acquired *him*, really. Or acquired rather care for his welfare. I think it is something Praisegod Norton would have wished."

"Ah! Corporal Norton. He was a good man. I liked him."

"Yes. We all did. He was going to get married. Did you know that? To the woman who is now our cook here."

"Go on!"

"You will meet her, I expect. You'll certainly taste her food, if you are staying. But what do you advise? About getting this man away?"

"There are ships in and out of Lynn, sir. Every day, someone goes somewhere. I think our best chance is Amsterdam, to the hollanders. I think you may find others have gone out through Lynn to get there. The hollanders' prince befriends them."

"His wife is King Charles' daughter."

"Is that right? God rot them all. Sorry. Anyway, I think it will not be difficult. There is a shipmaster who owes me certain... shall we say, obligations. He has some guilty secrets. He goes regularly to the hollanders' country. He has taken others."

"I know. Through Lynn. Through Parliament's own Lynn!"

"Oh yes. Under the very nose of Colonel Valentine Walton — you remember him, sir — and his garrison. Anyway, my friend David Humbold, the sea captain, will take him there, quiet, if I say he must. I'm sure of it."

"You must have advanced far in King's Lynn society, Simon, if this Humbold sea captain does your bidding."

"Well, sir. As you can imagine. We acquire information merely by hanging around the streets. And information brings influence, perhaps power. A word in an ear creates a willingness to do business. Humbold, well, he brings in cargoes only a part of which gets known to the exciseman. The rest goes out to the fences in the town, smooth like. Dave Humbold will take your man. Who is he, by the way? Or would you rather I did not know?"

"No, you can know." Josiah smiled at the irony. "It is George Chennery. He who you watched that time in Lynn."

"God's truth? That Cavalier! The blue coat with the pistols. Ha! Well, what goes around, comes around. So, now we need him covered and taken out of the country."

"We do. I do."

"Is Oliver Cromwell involved this time?"

"Er. No. I'd rather he did not know."

"Well, he won't be told by me or mine. God's truth, sir. You sure you know what you are doing?"

"No. All my instincts tell me I'm acting wrongly, but the alternative will make me feel *completely* wrong. If you follow."

"The alternative being to give this George Chennery up to Oliver Cromwell?"

Smart as always, Simon. "Yes."

"It'll cost money, sir. Oh, not for me. I'll do it for you for nothing... "

"No, Simon, I'll pay you. I don't want to be another person obliged to you."

"Ow! Sir! But, I accept that. A deal settled. But we'll have to pay for his passage. And I'll have to hide him in Lynn. Can you get him to Lynn? Leave it then to me. I reckon ten pounds should cover the job."

"That's good. I'll pay that. Now come and meet my father, and have some dinner with us."

"No sir. I'll eat in the kitchen, with the other..."

"No you will not, Simon. I'm making you a partner in this business. You are my guest. You'll stay the night too."

*

As the damage to the body of Sir George Chennery mended itself, he was able to converse with his hosts when they visited him. John Souter saw quickly that George would become bored, a condition that might perhaps produce some mischief, and so he took pleasure in showing what books they possessed to their guest. John fell to discussion of these with Endsleigh Seaton, discussion in which George joined, apparently willing to talk with his host, and the Puritan Parson. Perhaps he merely sought diversion while time lay heavy upon him.

John had proudly showed to George both Raleigh's *History*, a book that had been a treasure trove to Josiah in his early years, and Fox's *Book of Martyrs*, venerated then by most literate English households. George had, before this, read neither.

Of Fox's book, George said, "My mother had a copy. But I have not before read it. What a spirit possessed these men and women," he said, "that they should suffer so. And willingly!"

"Was your mother, then, for further reformation of the church," asked the Reverend Seaton.

"Oh, assuredly so."

The clergyman was handling Fox's book as something holy. He said, "How different matters were then, what... eighty years ago. No man then safely opposed the royal will in a matter of religion."

John said, "It possibly took Queen Mary by surprise that so many of her subjects espoused a creed that rejected her Pope."

"But all England subsequently formed its opinion of Roman Catholicism from the fact that she burned alive those that did." Endsleigh Seaton cradled the book. "To me, this book is trumped in its importance only by my Bible." Turning again to George, he said, "I had rather hoped that King Charles would fulfil your mother's wishes."

George said only, "You did?" He seemed surprised that anyone should have that hope.

"I did. Had he done so, his troubles would probably not have arisen."

"Sirs, you have been generous to me. I owe it to you both not to dissemble. I am not a man of any great faith. It seems to me that if God is, then He don't care much for us. He does not stop us killing and maiming each other. See how well we have done it." He indicated his damaged shoulder.

It was John Souter that saw the opportunity. "And that distresses you? That suffering?"

"It does. Yes. Not just suffering to me, but to all those others. There has been much pain."

"Then Sir George, may I say this? What you may be feeling is compassion, charity, love, for your neighbour who suffers. You are disappointed with the world. That is the root of your anger. And all we Christians offer the world is love, and the hopeful message that the world is redeemed by suffering."

George looked at the older man and read from his face that the Christian message allowed John Souter to make complete sense of a world that — when he thought on it — George himself found totally perplexing.

"I am of a melancholic disposition, sir. Melancholic."

John replied, "Sir, I think it my duty as your host not to press upon you my own opinion. I leave you to read more in Fox's book. Only leaven it with a reading too of Raleigh's 'History'. For continual thoughts of persecution and suffering may... dampen your spirits."

George was, after a period of some weeks able to rise from his bed and walk around the house, and into the farm. No one made any attempt to hide him. When Josiah had proposed that George should stay hidden, his father had dismissed the notion.

Josiah, however, concluded that it was time that George was away. It mattered little to him whether George was fit enough to withstand the rigours of the journey. What taxed him was how he was to get George, still weak, still looking wounded, bandaged and with his arm in a sling, the several miles to Lynn.

In the event, this was accomplished by allowing him to ride there, on Marigold, escorted by Josiah himself, riding Judgement.

They met the garrison of Lynn, as Josiah knew they would, some ten miles out from the town. On a bridge over the Ouse stood some red coated men, and Josiah could see a small queue of horsemen, carts and pedestrians being held up and examined. George said nothing, and, when their turn came, Josiah trotted out the story they had earlier agreed. He gave his name, and, indicating his companion, said, "This is my friend, and we go to Lynn so that he may consult Doctor Cooper there."

"Your friend looks to have an injury," said one of the soldiers, a huge fellow in a waistcoat of buff hide, stained by sweat and wear. "How came he by that?"

"At Colchester. He was there when Black Tom Fairfax was there." The implication was that George received his injuries under Sir Thomas Fairfax's command. But Josiah would not lie.

"Oh, aye? Was he indeed?" The big man looked at George, "but you do not say he was amongst the Godly."

No, indeed.

At that moment, an imperious voice rang out, "Captain Souter, as I live and breathe! Captain Souter. It *is* you, is it not?" Shouldering his way through the surrounding people came a tall officer. When Josiah had seen him last, this man had been an Ensign in Valentine Walton's regiment, and they had met, in Lynn, three years before. The officer addressed the big soldier.

"Thompson, what ails you? Do you not know a Parliamentary officer when you see one? I beg pardon, captain." He beckoned Josiah to draw away from the crowd and on over the bridge, walking alongside Judgement, and looking up. George was following. "Apologies if you were rudely handled, captain. We are still rounding up the malignant fugitives. We cannot be too careful."

Josiah to him gave the same account of himself and his companion, and their need to press on to Lynn. The officer was now only too eager to speed them on their way, "There is much that goes on that a simple infantry officer does not need fully to comprehend," he said as they parted, "You will be in Lynn tonight. Please speak well of us to Colonel Walton... That is, if you can." Josiah was content to allow the fellow to think that he himself was still engaged in the clandestine activity that had taken him to Lynn on the occasion of their original meeting.

The road to Lynn imposed no further impediment to them, and they moved swiftly. George was clearly in pain, his face was grey, and Josiah slowed their pace to ease matters.

Arriving in Lynn, Josiah put into effect the second part of his plan, and as arranged took George first to the substantial house of his acquaintance Doctor Cooper and, without any falsehood, asked the physician to examine and dress George's wounds.

Amongst the crowds in the streets of Lynn, there were the reddish-brown coats of the garrison, from Walton's regiment. There were also other units in their brighter red coats. Josiah therefore did not see Isaiah Yates amongst them all. But Isaiah saw him. He had watched at the gate. That meant that the arrival of Josiah's sickly companion had also been observed.

Josiah had left his companion with Doctor Cooper while he found *The Mermaid Inn*. Once contact had been made with Simon, the exercise was quickly progressed. An exhausted, and by now grey faced George was slickly whisked away.

Josiah found himself mightily relieved. He felt quite light-hearted.

He had no intention of drawing attention to himself by calling upon Valentine Walton, the town's governor. Rather, leading Marigold, he slipped back the way he had come, thinking to explain to the red-coated picquet on the bridge that his injured friend was left behind in the doctor's care. In the event, he found the soldiers absent, and so crossed the river unnoticed and took the road home.

*

Isaiah was saddened by his ex-commander's apparent apostasy to the great Cause they had both once served together, and to which he had thought Josiah had given himself without reservation. But Isaiah did not waste time in sentiment or retrospect. He, for the moment, dismissed Josiah's action from his mind. Perhaps, he thought, there were factors at work of which he — Isaiah — had no notion. And, since Isaiah knew where Josiah would be should further contact be required, Isaiah kept his eye only upon his prize.

A lieutenant from Elias Brydon's office could be sure of active support from Colonel Valentine Walton, and so a squad of soldiers was waiting at the quay. Isaiah thought he had only to deploy his own observers, and then await the identity of the vessel upon which the injured man was loaded.

Simon's gang, however, worked smoothly and inconspicuously. Humbold's ship, *Ariel's Kiss*, had already loaded her cargo, and awaited only one large roll of carpet. This having been carried aboard, she slipped from the wharf, working her way down river. Shortly afterwards, her sails tumbled from their furling, caught the wind and took her out to sea.

George had been prepared to accept the indignity of being concealed within the roll of carpet. He had seen the advantage — to him — of this necessity. Now, he recalled Doctor Cooper's advice that he should rest and he took to the hard basic bunk that furnished his tiny cabin. He decided that his voyage across the German Ocean would best be spent asleep.

*

"You were hiding him. You were concealing a malignant. *Here*." Isaiah confronted Josiah with the accusation. It was the truth. But unacceptably phrased.

"Not *concealing*. He came here a wounded man…"

"Your duty was to see him captured. Turned over to the army."

94

"Hush Isaiah!" Anger rose up in Josiah. "Hush. Listen to me. I will explain. George Chennery arrived here in Monks Soham, an injured man. We had not known he was to arrive. We had no warning. No one here invited him. We did not know at the time that he had been in Colchester fight. We did not then make the connection. Now, how would you have me behave if an injured man comes to my house? Tell me, as a Christian! What I did was not wrong. It was the Gospel. We took him in, we bound up his wounds. That was no felony, no misdemeanour. It was simple hospitality. Once a guest... you know the implications. There was then an obligation in honour." Josiah was the more annoyed as he recalled how his own misgivings — at the time — had been over-ruled.

"What of your obligation in honour to the Parliament? To the cause? To your oath? Or do those things no longer matter?"

"No, but I had an older and more compelling... an *overriding* obligation. The ancient and honourable rules of Christian hospitality! Remember the words our Lord Jesus Himself spoke: *For I was an-hungered and ye gave me meat; I was thirsty and ye gave me drink; I was a stranger and ye took me in... For verily, I say unto you, inasmuch as ye have done it unto one of the least of these my brethren, ye have done it unto me.* Matthew chapter twenty-five, Isaiah. And Hebrews chapter thirteen, Isaiah, *Be not forgetful to entertain strangers; for thereby some have entertained angels unawares.* Do *those* things no longer matter to you, Isaiah?"

They lapsed into silence. This was a new sensation: an awkwardness between them. Somehow, matters would, in the future, never be quite the same. That realisation raised a sadness in the hearts of both men.

Isaiah had arrived within the week of Josiah's trip to King's Lynn. He had asked for a formal meeting with Josiah — alone. Once they were together in the small room that passed as the office, containing a table, two chairs, the record books and not much else, Isaiah had come straight to the point. He was there, he said, to establish George Chennery's movements, and his route into Lynn and escape. He knew that Colonel Brydon would want him to have done no less. And, when he came to make his report, Brydon would want to know all Chennery's contacts, where he had been, with whom had he been meeting. That was the way, he knew, that Brydon worked, as he rooted out the last smouldering resistance to Parliament's victory.

But Isaiah could not see himself telling Brydon that ex-Ironside Captain Souter had now turned into a royalist activist. Not his old commander. He knew that was not so.

He said, "Well, Josiah, what will I report to Colonel Brydon? What I say may well become known to Oliver."

Josiah had calmed. He had a very genuine regard for his old comrade-in-arms. He was saddened at the genuine anguish he saw being displayed. Anguish which he had generated. And generated, he knew, in spite of his own better judgement. He suddenly remembered advice his mother had given him: "To thyself always be true." So long ago. It calmed him. "Well, Isaiah," he said, "it is not for me to tell you your duty. You know the truth."

"The truth may well lead to your arrest."

"I doubt that I will be punished."

Isaiah thought that was true. And yet... he knew of Parliamentary officers — the Pembroke Castle commanders, as an example — who had acted contrary to their oaths, had assisted the royalists in the late trouble. They were now on their way into exile.

"Josiah, What you may not realise is that George Chennery is in truth a key man in recent events. He is a conspirator, apparently in the closest way privy to the plans of the malignants, an intimate of their Prince Rupert. We kept our eye on him. We lost him. Then Maidstone went up in royal flames. Who was in Maidstone? *He* was. In the middle of it. *He made that happen.* Or helped in it. Where has he gone now? He has slipped away."

Josiah thought of George Chennery and what he knew of him. He had judged him a shallow man, and unlikely to have played any role of so much significance. He said, "George Chennery was in no fit state to cause any further trouble. The man's shoulder was ruined. He will never lift a sword again. Or shoot."

"His gift was intrigue and message carrying, Josiah. You do not need an able body to do that work."

"No, indeed. But, see here Isaiah. He is free, but you'll soon catch up with him. That Colonel Brydon, I have met him, and he will have a man — probably several men, if I judge him right — with Prince Rupert even now. You'll pick up the trail."

Isaiah noted that Josiah spoke of "you" not "we", but that merely saddened him further.

Josiah finished, "Then you are back on his trail and he'll lead you to the next lot of trouble."

"I notice you speak as if you are no longer amongst us. You speak in a mightily detached way about the fortunes of the cause. Why is that? What has happened to you?"

Josiah thought of the visit from that young Cornet who came looking for George that day the soldiers had visited his house. Josiah remembered his arrogance.

"I no longer have the same certainties, Isaiah."

"You would not see the King restored?"

"He has not been removed. King Charles is our King yet. And nothing you achieve in the field alters that, Isaiah. He remains the King."

Josiah found himself thinking too of Susanna.

Isaiah brought him back to the matter in hand. "Yes," he said. "And so, if King Charles cannot see the judgements of God given in the field — cannot or perhaps *will* not — then we will do without such a king."

"Oh Isaiah! I find that a difficulty. For, without him and without the crown, how will we find legitimacy? How will the law function, how will the courts? For if we abandon the law, what protects this," he waved his hands indicating his property, "what protects me? And you?"

"This", said Isaiah, tapping the great sword he held between his knees. "this protects us. Wielded by the God-fearing."

"Ah yes," said Josiah. And he remembered again the pistol he had laid before the Mayor of King's Lynn. That Mayor had been a contemptible creature, but what he had said upon that occasion was true. Of the pistol, he had said *that is not authority, that is power*. He had been right. Praisegod had been there then. That was in the summer of 1645, the summer in which Praisegod had died.

"I see nothing in front of us except endless struggle. Endless fighting." Josiah was become decidedly morbid.

"No. We shall have one more big fight. That'll be the end of them."

"And if they win…"

"God will not suffer that! God will not let England suffer as you fear. Be of good cheer. We are the masters now."

"So, what *will* you report? Tell the truth, Isaiah. The truth will not let you down. Now, we will have dinner together. We will share all your news. Father will take great delight in your company. As do I. Except when you unjustly upbraid me. But you remain welcome. You are our only visitor nowadays."

The question was left unanswered.

*

Colonel Brydon was in fact told that George Chennery had indeed been sheltered at Monks Soham. And by Josiah Souter. Isaiah had no alternative. For unless he could adequately account for the weeks George Chennery had spent recovering in Josiah's home, it would have appeared that he, Isaiah, had been engaged in an uncharacteristically unenterprising and fruitless mission. Isaiah knew that if he reported that he had *not* established George's movements, some other spy would be sent to get to the truth. That truth was not so very difficult to root out. He had decided to explain Josiah's motive to Elias Brydon.

"Captain Souter had no knowledge that Sir George was a Royalist soldier, sir. There was no collusion, merely the arrival in Monks Soham of an injured man, and Christian charity and hospitality given."

He added, "Josiah Souter remains committed to the cause."

Elias Brydon looked at Isaiah and knew his unease with his own words. But he also judged that Isaiah was not concealing a traitor, merely covering an unwise indiscretion. He said, "Well, Isaiah, of course there *may* be injured men wandering the county of Suffolk who have not met those injuries at Colchester fight. But I doubt that."

"When he arrived, sir, when Sir George arrived at Monks Soham, they had no news of Colchester."

"They knew there was a siege. Of that, I have no doubt."

"Yes. But thought all royalists still shut up within the town, sir."

"Perhaps."

The interview had ended without Isaiah really knowing whether he had settled the matter, or whether he had made great trouble for the Souter household. He thought sadly the probability that the latter was the case, and vexed with his own performance.

As he walked away, he muttered to himself, "I should have lied. *I should have lied.*"

10. Mixed Fortunes

They had congratulated themselves. In the whole of that four-hour fight into Preston, and the pursuit that destroyed the Scots invasion, the army itself lost only one hundred lives. This was seen as a great deliverance.

Death claimed many of the Scots. The Parliament sent commissioners and there was an attempt to find out if each Scots soldier was a pressed man or a volunteer. It was the latter, those who had chosen to make war, which were sent off to the Sugar Islands. They went, effectively, as slaves, and all men knew how the Sugar Islands treated white men. Pressed men, judged to be those who had had no choice in the matter, went home. It was a rough justice, very rough.

But death struck too, nearer home.

Colonel Nathaniel Musgrave's regiment marched back to Bristol. There were rumours of forces required in Scotland, and in Ireland, but Bristol had to be garrisoned, and so back they went. The pace of their return south was a little kinder than that trek to Preston, but they were there within ten days. As Sergeant Hollin said, "If Oliver goes to Scotland, we can be back up there in a fortnight."

In fact, Oliver Cromwell made Scotland wait. He was busy in London, as were all the leaders of Independency. There was some work to be done to safeguard what had been achieved. Colonel Pride, in particular was to become famous in London at this time. He and his troops excluded from their seats in the Parliament those who might make difficulties in the great work to which the Grandees of the army now applied themselves.

It may have been — as Noah came to believe — that wet march into Lancashire, or perhaps just the requirement, after the Preston fight, to keep moving. Perhaps it came from the Scots. Dysentery hit Musgrave's. A consequence was that men began to fall out as they came south.

The first symptom was the uncoiling in their bellies of a terrible pain, and then uncontrollable bowels, the liquid pouring out of them tinted red, so that the disease was known as 'the bloody flux'. The surgeons could only instruct that the sick men — and some women — were gathered into groups, to be effectively abandoned, left to the dubious care of villages and towns through which they passed. Water was dispensed, if they were lucky, because it was dehydration that killed them – the surgeons had come to understand that. But as to the cause, they never knew, nor did they have any cure.

Noah watched men fall out in front of him, and prayed that his own file would not be touched. Indeed, it was strange to him how apparently random the bloody flux could be. It would take here one man, leaving for the moment his closet companions to march on. But then another complete file of six would fall away within a mile or two of each other, clutching their stomachs, and casting away musket and kit to rush to relieve themselves. Some just collapsed upon the road and a cart at the rear was picking some up.

By the time they reached Bristol, 200 men, one quarter of the regiment, had gone.

The remainder looked at each other, wondering when the symptoms would strike their mates or themselves. The anxiety was palpable.

Captain Parker was visibly shaken. He developed the idea that his men should wash. This was a novelty to many, but he made it an order and they marched into the Severn and obeyed him. He also superintended more closely what was cooked and what they ate. Again, he advised that food preparation and consumption should be preceded by a washing of the hands. It was a fact that, once back in Bristol, and subject to this regime, the rate at which his company was affected diminished. No one really attributed it to his actions, which were merely seen as eccentric.

The bloody flux took away little Mark Golightly. He had so manfully shouldered his duty over the entire year, that Noah had thought him indestructible. But one night, Mark said quietly "Oh! sweet Jesus," and began the run for the latrines which marked the onset of the disease. Three days later they buried him.

It took too Moses Marsh, despite his great strength. As he lay dying, Rebecca was beside him, weeping quietly and with a rag wiping away the sweat that marked his tussle with the destroying wastage of his tough body. "I cannot lose you," wept Rebecca, but she did. Moses lay, in his end, as if he had merely slept. He too went into the pit where the latest casualties were laid.

Moses was amongst the last to go. That time. The flux came less often to claim victims after it took tough Moses Marsh. Then came the day that no one died. And men started to look into each other's faces with new hope, new interest. "Keep washing those hands," said Captain Parker. "And give thanks to God."

For what? thought Noah. Then he corrected himself. *No, the Captain is right. I was not taken. Give thanks. Praise the Lord. Praise the Lord always. Rejoice, again, I say, rejoice.* He thought it sounded so hollow. He wondered what had happened to him. He felt less certain, somehow.

Noah went to find Rebecca. She was sitting on the ground, hugging her knees, weeping. He sat beside her. They were looking over the burial ground, and the freshly turned earth showed where Moses lay, with the others.

He put an arm around Rebecca's shoulders. They stayed still for a long time.

*

Phoebe had hatched a plan. She awaited her moment.

One short dark winter day, she told Susanna that one of the chickens was trapped within the stable loft. She told her friend, untruly, that she could hear a clucking that suggested the bird was in distress. She affected distraction.

"I have a pie to finish, I have no time..."

The chickens were one of the two women's' particular cares, and they prided themselves upon the eggs. Susanna therefore set off to the stables, and up the ladder into the loft.

Of course, Phoebe knew that Josiah was already up there, struggling to mend a hole in the roof, caused by a persistently dislodged slate. It was a job better done from the exterior, but the fetching of ladders, and the danger of the slates of the roof on a cold day had deterred him, making him tackle the job from the inside.

Susanna had gone up the ladder and then stood silently looking at Josiah's back as he stood on a stool, working awkwardly up against the slope of the roof.

Josiah, having slid the slate back into place, stepped down, turned and found himself facing her. Both knew that there was no one anywhere near.

Josiah's thoughts were hot and fast. *She is here. There will never again be such an opportunity. Now, Josiah, on, on. There can be no error.* He saw her mouth. He saw her eyes. Her shoulders, her breasts. *Tell her. Tell her.*

But words he could not find. There was a great lump in his throat. A dryness. He just held out his arms. He thought, *I am here, and I am yours.*

He was bewitched, and if he afterwards thought on why, he would always identify her eyes as the magic. They were almond shaped, large lidded, brown ; her eyelashes thick and dark. Her dark hair cascaded around her shoulders.

Susanna could only think, *Mine, come now to me. Tell me you are mine. Nothing else. Please do not hesitate.* Some of this must have showed upon her face.

In her mind there arose the thought that she was home now, and safe. This was not a man that would depart. He was honesty incarnate. Integrity. She knew too that she had conquered him; that breeding, status, principles, had all until then restrained him, but she had overcome them all. And she adored him. She looked at his strong face, the chin and mouth, the eyes. Nothing, she knew, would take her away. Ever. Except death, except death. "Oh my love, my love," she said.

She did not fly into his open arms, but rather moved slowly and quietly towards him. Nonetheless, there was no hesitation: it was as if she was savouring the moment. He folded her into his embrace, looked briefly at those great, gorgeous eyes, and then fastened his lips over hers. He was consumed by the passion that dictated to his arms and lips. He wanted to grind her body into his, to absorb and possess her.

She felt a pent-up heat, as gates long closed, opened in her mind and in her body. Her passion was for possession of him, and she clung on to him, opening her mouth, exchanging breath for breath, and only aware that her head was possessed with ecstasy.

It was hours later when Ebenezer, entering the room below, awoke them to complete darkness. "Master Josiah, are you up there. Old Master says dinner is awaiting 'ee. Said you were up there roofing."

Josiah said quickly. "Yes, Ebenezer, I'll be down." He put his arms again around Susanna, and hugged her and kissed her. He got to his feet, and held out his hand to her. She shook her head, waved her hands,

102

mouthed 'No, no. You go.' But he would have none of that. He said quietly to her, "I am not ashamed. Are you?"

Ebenezer was therefore treated to the sight of first Josiah and then Susanna descending towards him down the loft ladder. There was hay in their hair, and a joy on their faces. Ebenezer did not know what to do or say, and, red faced, ambled out of their way, not displeased, not disapproving, just confused.

Old John was therefore not the first to know, although Josiah made sure that he was the first to hear of it from his own lips. He came to the dinner table, still with some few slips of hay in his hair, and said to his father.

"It is Susanna, father. She and I know."

His father clapped his hands. "Praise to the Lord. Alleluia! You will be married then?"

"I rather think that I married her this afternoon."

"Josiah!" His father said, but indulgently, and thinking, *Not before time, my son.*

*

What took Josiah by surprise was an absence of guilt at what he had done. He had been told by his Bible that fornication was a sin, and that sin grieved his God. He had fallen mightily. All his breeding and upbringing pointed him towards condemnation of himself. He expected to feel overwhelming remorse. But this eluded him. It got to the point that he said to himself that the absence of guilt must be a sure sign of a fall from grace. He said as much to his father. John, since that first announcement, had not ceased to exult over the liaison, which was the union of the two people he held most dear.

"You feel so because your intentions are honourable, Josiah. You love her. There is no room for guilt. Not where there is real love. You intended to make her yours, and you are hers. Marry. And marry soon."

Whatever plans were hatched about a wedding, they were interrupted by a summons delivered by an army galloper. The letter the man brought reminded Josiah that, even if he had resigned his commission, he was bound still by his oath. In obedience to that he was to report without delay to the office of Colonel Brydon, whose signature ended this unwelcome intrusion. It reminded him sharply that there was still trouble in England that touched him. He realised too that now he wanted only to be left alone, at peace in Monks Soham.

*

"I understand you know Sir George Chennery."

Josiah did not feign surprise. He knew Elias Brydon would be quick to see any pretence. Besides, he had decided, as he had advised Isaiah, that the truth was the best course to follow.

"I first met George Chennery when I took a cook from his house."

Brydon raised an eyebrow. He had not known of that early connection. "That was when?"

"In the summer of 'forty six. The Lieutenant-General received a letter from that person, and he himself passed it to me. My employment of her was a debt of honour I owed to Corporal Praisegod Norton. You remember Corporal Norton, Colonel? You will recall he and I were instrumental in settling affairs at King's Lynn."

Brydon nodded slowly several times. He said, "You then met George Chennery again."

And Josiah in his honesty confirmed the report Isaiah had made. His answer covered also his motivation. Brydon became decidedly unsympathetic. His words made Josiah increasingly uncomfortable.

"There has been sequestration for those who have betrayed the Cause. Ex-officers... Mister Souter, you need to understand how deeply wounded the cause was in the recent troubles. Men who were trusted... Men who had served alongside us earlier... were now in arms against us. In arms against the judgements of God. Men once judged staunch for the Parliament now out for the King. And you will know that if one man becomes such a turncoat, there are more who might take no such action, but in their heart supported Charles Stuart. Those men, sit at home perhaps, but work ill against the cause. They perhaps shelter the fugitive malignant..."

"Colonel Brydon, I am not false."

"Possibly not. I might think you are not. Others may deduce otherwise. For this reason I give you an opportunity to put beyond all doubt your loyalty. Otherwise..."

"Otherwise?"

"A report will have to be made. It will include your name and an account of the shelter you have given to a well-known malignant, a *leading* malignant. It will be seen by appropriate men, the committee of the Parliament that judges whether there is, or is not to be... *further action.*"

Josiah was angry. But he knew this was not the moment to express that. Did it mean nothing that he had spent three years in the Parliament's army? Under the command of those who now directed the affairs of the kingdom. Had they no loyalty to him? Apparently not. He kept silent.

"The younger Charles Stuart, who some will call the Prince of Wales, is presently in France. He will come again into this kingdom. He will come soon. This is what you must do. You will find George Chennery — again. He will know the Prince's plans. You will seek to discover where the young Charles Stuart is likely to come. If you find that out, you will tell me. Until you do have that conversation with me, I will take no further action on the matter we have just discussed. You will be released from any further obligation to me when we have had that conversation."

"Why should George Chennery tell me that sort of news? That would surely be critical to the success of any military operation."

"Ha! No, that is not the way it works. You masquerade as a sympathiser. Charles Stuart wants every man turned. It will be no secret. His appearance will be promised here and there to bring out his supporters."

"Then how do you know what I might be told can possibly be accurate?"

"Mister Souter, you are not my only source. I have already received notice of several places at which Charles Stuart is expected. Your report will be one of many, but from the many we build a picture of the probable truth."

"And I may presume, Colonel," said Josiah, "that no one's information will match in its likely accuracy information from Sir George Chennery."

"Precisely."

"Where should I start looking for Sir George do you think, Colonel?"

"Try Heathcote House. It is in Northamptonshire — but you will know that. Your ... er, cook. George Chennery arrived there two days ago." Colonel Brydon smiled at Josiah's surprised face. "Oh yes, he is returned."

*

And so, for the second time in his life, Josiah came to Heathcote House. Arriving, he was taken by surprise at his reception. It happened as he approached the gates to the park, having not yet left the highway. It happened so suddenly that there was no possibility of avoiding it.

A man stepped out from the bushes at the roadside and presented at him two levelled pistols. As he halted, another appeared, suddenly close, beside Josiah's right side, seizing Judgement's bridle. There had been no warning, no possibility of avoiding this.

The man at Judgement's head laid his own hand over the holster concealing one of Josiah's pistols, to discourage any thought of resistance.

Josiah saw himself to be a prisoner. Presumably of bandits, highwaymen.

"In the name of the Parliament of England..." he began.

"Shut your mouth!" said the man with the two pistols. Judgement's head was turned and he was led off to one side of the road, the path pressing through unbroken waist high ferns and bracken. After several minutes, they passed through a gap that had been torn in a wall, entering, Josiah thought, the park of Heathcote House. Here there were great trees, and under the trees the ground was clearer. Josiah was turning in his mind what manner of ambuscade this had been, he had thought these were merely robbers. They would turn out the saddlebags and then... But a greater anxiety came into his mind; what if these men knew of his mission, and were not mere highwaymen, but were out for the King?

His worst fears seemed to be confirmed when Judgement was led forward and opening before him he looked down into a distinct dell in the woodland. He saw ahead a small and rather weak fire, and beside it several other men. The faces all looked towards him. Several strode quickly forward to assist his captors. *Five, six... eight*, he counted silently.

One man remained beside the fire, but facing them, his hands upon his hips. He had on a short cloak, and a well feathered hat. A glance sufficed for Josiah to recognise his quality. Instinctively he knew him as these brigands' chief.

The man said, "Well, who do we have here?" He spoke with the clipped accent of the aristocracy. Then, "we'll have the content of his bags, and, I think..." he moved closer to Judgement, "we'll have the horse."

A figure came from the back of the group. He moved without vigour, a tired and injured figure, his shoulder crooked, maimed.

"No," he said, "we will not do that."

Josiah recognised with astonishment that the intervention was from George Chennery. He said nothing.

"Well met, Mister Souter."

George Chennery turned to the man in the feathered hat. "This is Mister Souter of Suffolk. And we will not be detaining him long. I have a great debt of honour to Mister Souter. He is..."

"We all have had friends on the other side, George."

"Mister Souter will not acknowledge me as his friend, I think. No, my debt to him is greater. Greater than friendship. You will release him, now." George looked meaningfully at the man who held Judgement's head, who did as he was told.

Josiah thought, *not brigands, then*. Realising that his captors were royalist soldiers, he thought fast. 'What can I do that will disarm them?' He dismounted. He looped Judgement's reins over his arm, and stood to await developments.

George Chennery came closer. "I never really had the opportunity properly to thank you Mister Souter, for getting me away that time in King's Lynn. I do so now. That was a great service."

Josiah noted that George looked ill. His face was grey and sweaty. Josiah thought that he had hardly had time to recuperate from his injuries. And those injuries had been severe, he recalled. He managed, "I am astonished to see you, sir, once again at large in Northamptonshire."

George smiled. "Oh, yes. The fox has broken cover again, Mister Souter. There is work to do. Of a kind."

"Is there?"

"I regret to break in upon this intimacy, George," it was the feathered hat that spoke, "but we will have the horse at least."

George turned upon him and said quietly, "No, my lord."

The man raised an eyebrow. George went on. "I will defend Mister Souter's liberty and his property, if necessary with my life. And you will recall that you require me to explain to... others... why you are now.... what you are, and that you will need me there when you meet them."

How intriguing, thought Josiah. The one with the feathered hat conceded the point and turned away, making light of his defeat. He returned to stand beside the fire. His followers all seemed, for the moment, to have lost interest in their erstwhile captive.

George motioned to Josiah to move and they walked back towards the road, leading Judgement. As they went, George said, "Why are you here?"

"I came to look for you."

"So, you are *not* in fact astonished?"

"No. Well, yes. I expected that I might here get news of you. But, to find you in residence in your own home."

"Ah! Well, I am sorry that I cannot entertain you here as you were good enough to accommodate me in Suffolk. But we are on campaign, and we are not going to get trapped within the house when your Parliament friends arrive. So, we bivouac here, in the park. Where we have room to manoeuvre. But you will understand that, being a cavalryman yourself. And," he added, "of course, we watch the road."

There was a pause. Then George said again, "Why are you here?"

With an effort of will, Josiah began his lie. "I wish to know where I must go in order to be of use to the King. I am thinking that his cause will... *must*... resurrect itself, that there is still fighting to be done. Where should I go, who should I join? I thought the Prince of Wales might come again. Should I await him? I thought you would know. I came to ask you."

George Chennery looked at him, as if not quite hearing correctly. He said, "This is a change. How has this come to be? I admit there are several — many — men who were friends of the Parliament that now have come into their senses. Some of them turned out at Maidstone, at Colchester and with the Scots. You are in good and great company. My advice to you, for the moment is to go home, Mister Souter. Await news. If you are serious, I will get word to you when you might be of some service."

Josiah was committed to his falsehood. George Chennery continued his close observation of this erstwhile Roundhead. Josiah gave him look for look. Josiah was suppressing a wish to scream at his own charade. George was trying to pierce any dishonesty, to perceive whether what was being said was true. Not for the first time, Josiah's open and straight face carried conviction. He said, "Surely, the King being no longer free, the Prince of Wales must act for him. He will come, will he not? And soon."

"The Prince is in France. He is with his mother. No secret was made of his departure." George was saying nothing new.

"Should I go to Ireland? Will we seek the King's fortunes there?"

George Chennery smiled. "Ireland will be the mess it always is. Men will fight there, yes. Probably they are fighting already. Does killing ever stop in Ireland? But it is not — never will be — the place in which to seek a decision. You would be wasted there."

Josiah felt his arm gripped. George was still looking at his face, his body close, and speaking with intensity. "Now, Mister Souter, you tell *me* something. The King is, as you have said, no longer free. They have him close, your friends in the Parliamentary army. What will *they* do, do you think? How will they go forward? What have you heard?"

It was Josiah's turn now to look deliberately at the other man's face, keeping his own feelings masked. He thought quickly. It was a matter made public by that news-sheet. He said, "There is to be a great public trial. The King will be accused like some criminal. The accusation is that the king persists in the struggle..."

"In the face of the judgements of God. Yes, I know," said George. He had read in Josiah's face dismay at the implication of what he had been forced to say. He said, "Mister Souter, they will put the King on trial. There is nothing the King's servants can do about that. We are broken. There is no direction of our affairs, no money, no troops, no... will."

"And the outcome will be?" Josiah could not — still — wholly comprehend the enormity of what his real friends might be being planning.

"Oh, the court involved — if you can call it that — will pretend to convict His Majesty. I know that."

"How can that be?"

"We are not dealing with lawfulness, Mister Souter. This is a matter of judicial murder. Oh yes. They will murder our monarch, under a form of law. It will break the power of the Crown in this land. That is their intention."

"And then?" Josiah had understood that these matters would proceed exactly in this way, but he had never before had a conversation that developed the idea to its conclusion.

"Then, Mister Souter, there will be such an enormous outpouring of grief and rage across this kingdom that your army friends will be swept away. Your Fairfax and your Cromwell will not be able to stand against the forces their action will unleash. It would be as well, at that moment, if you were active in the service of your King. My guess is that when that retribution carries all before it, those who merely sit at home will suffer. But, for now go home, Mister Souter, and wait."

"We will both serve King Charles, then…"

"Yes. King Charles the Second. For by my oath, the first of that name is sadly finished. But, in his going, he will cause us to triumph."

"Will the Prince of Wales wait for his father's death? Will he not attempt something now? Something to rescue him?" Josiah was outside Brydon's brief now, behaving with quite genuine engagement in the issue before them.

"He will be being advised that if he attempts anything, that will push matters to extremes. Most of his advisers will be unable to comprehend that King Charles is already as good as dead. That is only known to desperadoes such as you and I! When the King is killed then they will launch him."

George seemed contemptuous of those about the young Prince. "Most of those about him are Scotsmen. And the King is a Stuart King, remember. Your Parliamentary friends do not rule Scotland. They will launch him into Scotland. When the moment comes."

Josiah remembered his mission. "Scotland! Should I go to Scotland then?"

George laughed again, but not with any merriment. "No, Mister Souter. Do not go to Scotland. At least, not alone! They would cut your throat for a heretic. Go home. Wait there."

"And you?"

"I *am* home, Mister Souter."

Josiah remembered that Brydon knew Chennery was here. Without thinking, he said, suddenly, "They will be watching for you here. The army."

"Oh yes. That is required. I am to be noticed." George smiled. "We seek to remind the army, Parliament, Cromwell, whoever needs reminding, that we are yet a power in this land and that moving against the sacred person of His Majesty is not a good idea. I am used to that..." He saw an enquiry arise in Josiah's face. "I mean that I am used to being sent on fools' errands. Being sent here is yet another one! I cannot see my being here will in any way intimidate Old Ironsides."

"I hope you will recover your health." Josiah remembered the broken body in the guest room at Monks Soham. He found himself genuinely wishing health to this man, this Cavalier.

"I am of a despondent disposition, and the hurt compounds my despair, Josiah." He used the informal name. "I am lost."

They looked at each other, and each realised that what had grown between them in their several encounters was a mutual regard.

"May God bless you then," said Josiah, and offered his hand. George took it, smiling at the words. They stood for a moment, and then Josiah climbed onto Judgement's back. He saluted George, turned his horse south, back the way he had come, and went off. He urged Judgement forward to greater effort, and accelerating away, left George beside the road.

*

There was a wedding ceremony. It had to wait until after the Christmas feast, because the season of Advent would not permit the celebration. Endsleigh Seaton was old-fashioned enough to think this right.

But before that event, Susanna had, at John's insistence, taken her place at his table as his daughter-in-law. He had no problem with the change. He saw his life immeasurably enriched.

The staff of the house had some adjustments to make as Susanna became the "young master's wife." Phoebe was asked to make no change at all, since Susanna and she saw eye-to-eye in most things, and Susanna did not see her new role as an escape from work. There might need to be an adjustment in responsibilities, in deference, but that would wait.

After the wedding, all awkwardness overcome, they all thought that they would settle together well.

And so they would have done, had not dramatic news reached them. The next news-sheet that they saw announced the trial and the execution of the King.

Parliament – or rather the leadership of the militant Independents – had assembled as a High Court of Justice, had gone through the semblance of a trial, and had then judicially cut off the King's head.

In Monks Soham, the idea of King Charles being God's deputy had never taken hold. So the more exaggerated exclamations of horror that arose elsewhere in the country, were absent. But there was a sharp shock, as if a collective intake of breath, at the enormity of what had been done.

Old John Souter felt it keenly, so that the pleasure of the wedding was effaced in his mind. "The Parliament has called up this idea of democracy, that the people are sovereign, but the first public act of the Parliament men makes them anathema to all Englishmen. The people will never forgive them! To kill the King... What were they thinking! No one will support them now. They have forfeit the support of everyone. Now they will struggle to find legitimacy. They will struggle to find support. And they will know that if they appeal to the people — the people, who they say are sovereign — the people will turf them out."

Josiah was thinking of the men he knew. Men alongside whom he had been a soldier: Oliver Cromwell, Edward Whalley, Thomas Harrison. He said, "But it was a brave act. It took courage."

His father could not understand his temporising. "They have never lacked courage. These men. But the kingdom will now never be settled."

"Well, perhaps not so easily as if King Charles had accepted the judgements of God shown through battlefields." Josiah said crossly. He wanted to add the question, *what else could they have done?*, but he held his peace. He remembered George Chennery's prediction.

"No. Indeed. And Josiah," said Susanna, "People will struggle now, wont they, to find any legitimacy in whatever the Parliament does?"

"Aye" added old John Souter, "And — you mark my words — there will be a reaction. The pendulum will swing back. You think we can now have our religious freedom — but now there will come soon.... intolerance. You think the Presbyterian interest quiet — I tell you we have not heard the last of them! Nor the Royal party. Give it ten years. Ten years we will have of Parliamentary experiments. But legitimacy will never be found."

Susanna was prescient. "It will be ten years of tyranny. Ten years of rule by the army."

"And all because of this... stupid act of regicide." John Souter was showing weariness. Was it just his age, or something more fundamental? "And after that we shall have a King back. You mark my words. England will only find herself again when we have a King."

"But it was a brave act. It took courage." Josiah had the last word. He had heard enough. He went outside and across to the stables. He wanted to be with Judgement.

11. The Crowning Mercy

The household at Monks Soham was changing. The casual observer might look at the old gabled house and think that nothing was altered, but over the next two years the passage of time affected the inhabitants.

John Souter aged: by the summer of 1651 he was very much less active as a landowner and farmer. Age was stiffening his joints, and bending his bones. He continued functioning as the squire and magistrate, and his eyes remained bright, his mind sharp. But he rose less early, leaving almost entirely to his son the management of their farm. He still loved his dogs, and his walk each evening around the farm. On these occasions, Hepzibah still padded alongside him.

Susanna had not disappointed. Within months of the wedding, a son was born. They named him Oliver. At least, Josiah did. "It proclaims your opinions to the world," said Susanna, but not in disapproval. Delighting in his grandson, her father-in-law was only too pleased to spend hours minding the child, then joining in the development of his character and his education. When the news of Worcester fight came, the child was nearly two years old.

After reporting to Elias Brydon what he had discovered from George Chennery — that the Prince of Wales would come to Scotland — Josiah had never heard again from the army of Parliament. Brydon had merely said, "yes, it all fits," and that had closed the matter. Sensing that there was now little interest in him, Josiah had hurried away before anybody's mind changed. His sole purpose was now his new wife and his family, and his activity in managing their farm. These concerns absorbed him wholly, and he gave little thought to the wider affairs of the country. These intruded little into his life. He read the news-sheets that arrived so frequently, and sometimes discussed these with his father and wife over their dinner. But he felt no need for more active involvement in the affairs about which he was reading. His life as a Suffolk farmer now seemed to be a perfection of anything he had ever thought he might be. He had no ambition beyond the prolongation of his current situation. His contentment embraced the household.

The faith that had driven him to fight the King continued to be, for him, very real. He read the Bible alongside his father each evening. He thought of himself, still, as amongst 'the Elect'. His relationship with His God was his own mainspring. But God had ceased to demand that Josiah seek by warfare the further reformation of the English church, for no one any longer forbade him to worship in a way that he chose. No one any longer forced him into Sunday attendance in the parish church by the imposition of any fine. Strangely perhaps, the entire household now *wanted* to be there, because their vicar had chosen to advance the reformation locally, and in close liaison with his Squire, John Souter, had installed in the lovely old building a veritable new Jerusalem. The best reformed practice now flourished at Monks Soham, and the writ of Bishop and Archdeacon no longer ran there. But then, there were no longer bishops in England: the Parliament had abolished the office.

Susanna had thought that might be her biggest challenge, the acceptance of her new family's religiosity. But no, she was delighted to find that her preconception of Puritanism was misleading: the Souters' faith was overt, but so was their kindness, their love, which she saw sprang from the certainties on which they built their lives. There was frequent laughter, conviviality — wine every evening — and a ready welcome to the wandering fiddlers and pipe players who, in return for a night's board and lodging played for them of an evening.

Charlie was now in his youth, with all the awkwardness that can embarrass those years as boys develop into men. He was, of course immensely proud that his status was now the stepson of Josiah, and the Souters included him fully within the new family circle. He chose, however, to stay close to the ageing Ebenezer, and saw his entire future in the care of horses. Josiah did not push him into anything else, and Susanna did not ask it. "He will always be his father's son," she said, as if all was thus accounted for and complete.

All in all, it was a contented and joyous household that welcomed Isaiah Yates one evening in that summer, two and a half years after the execution of the King. He looked tired, indeed exhausted, and having dismounted in the yard, stood for a moment, his hands still upon his horse, his head resting on the saddle, as if stiff and full of discomfort. Josiah was quickly out of the house and into the yard to greet him, and noted the effort his friend put into turning and moving towards him.

"I have been too long in the saddle," Isaiah said ruefully.

"Yes. It is time you went home and stayed there," rejoined Josiah.

"No, I meant that I have ridden in the last few weeks the length and breadth of England. The army has made me move too far too fast. You are right. I am old and they do not deserve me. Not any more. Anyway, England does not need me. Not any longer. Not after Worcester fight."

"Yes. We were just reading the news-sheet that tells us all about it. Come in, Isaiah."

Isaiah had timed his arrival well, and dinner was set in front of him. Phoebe continued her mastery of the kitchen, and Susanna had not yet managed to impose upon her even a discussion about menus. It was a game pie that Isaiah enjoyed.

"Well, Josiah," said Isaiah, "you chose then, not to involve yourself in this latest how-d'ye-do? I hear men were out for King Charles in Norfolk."

"Oh holy angels!" said Josiah. "I went off in support of Oliver. Because he asked us all. But the farthest we in the Suffolk militia got was Hitchin. When we got to Hitchin, we were all sent home."

Susanna was silently watching the two men. She knew that Isaiah had an eye on Josiah's motivation. This caused her some unease. Was he a true friend? Was he here merely to break a journey?

"Where are you bound, Mister Yates?" she asked.

Isaiah answered her, but he looked at Josiah as he spoke. "King's Lynn, Mistress. I am sent there to make sure royalist fugitives do not get out through the port. We know they do, sometimes."

Old John was keen for news. "Tell us about Worcester, Isaiah. Were you there?"

"We all were, sir. Oliver had every trooper and red coat he could summon. And the militia. It is a glorious ending…"

"Is it ended then?" This from Josiah.

"The King of Scots is running. He will be captured. Like as not he'll share his father's fate. Anyone in England who thinks to espouse his rotten bankrupt side is now either dead, captured or fled abroad. He has no money, and no prospect of any. His Scots kingdom is now devoid of a defence, since it lies dead around Worcester. Oh yes, I think it is ended."

"I hope you are right."

"I am, Josiah. We won. Rejoice!"

"I will for tonight. I raise a glass. To the Commonwealth of England." Josiah proposed, but in his heart he was not joyous. It should have done, but it brought him no great pleasure.

"To this great victory for God and His saints!" Isaiah was quite carried away. "Oliver thinks it is done, Josiah. He called it ...*The crowning mercy* — Worcester fight — *the crowning mercy*."

"Well, he should know," said Susanna, looking at Josiah and sensing in him some shadow over the matter.

"What did it was the Scots," said Isaiah. "You know that England, I mean the people, were... lukewarm towards this commonwealth idea, this experiment with no king. Charles Stuart, the younger, came amongst us expecting the English to get up and march him triumphantly to his throne in London. Yes, I think he did. But look at what happened. He appeared at the head of an army of foreigners. An invader. So we — the commonwealth men... Oliver ... we appear as the national champions of England. Some malignants might have got out of bed to fight for Charles Stuart, but they would not stir themselves to help a Scots invasion. So, you see, the Scots delivered us, saved us a deal of trouble."

"Were there many killed?" asked old John. He had seen his own son ride off to war.

"Here's the hand of God, sir. We lost just two hundred souls. The nation delivered and only two hundred dead. Is that not something wonderful?"

Not for those men, thought Susanna. *Nor their widows.*

Isaiah was pressing on. "The Scots put up a tough fight, sir. And of course, there were English with them too, amongst the horse."

"And the Scots...?"

"We thought the King's army sixteen thousand, sir. They are no more."

"All dead?" asked Susanna. Josiah remembered that her first husband was such a casualty.

"No. Many are prisoners."

"Being sold as slaves, no doubt," interjected Josiah. "I can just believe that! There will be Parliament men crowding to buy the prisoners. And just to enrich further the already rich, to send them to the Sugar islands. Once there, may God have mercy upon them. What grief, what sadness."

"Josiah, it was necessary. The Scots are now unlikely to repeat their effort to impose the Presbytery upon us."

"I hope that England can enjoy its new freedom, Isaiah."

Isaiah was alarmed at his tone, "Why is there now such gloom and despondency in your heart? Is this not all that we set out to achieve? Why did we take up arms at first? We wanted, did we not, to establish Independency. We fought to give it life. That has been achieved."

"Which of us fully saw the end, Isaiah. When we set out, did we even comprehend the end to which we have come? No, we did not."

"No, because we thought that since we feared God, so did every other man. But they did not. The King did not. Had he done so, matters might have resolved themselves differently."

"The King serves my argument. A man who thought he knew the will of God. Thought God willed that he should triumph. God disposed otherwise. Can we be certain that this triumph of ours is so divinely intended? Can we?"

"Yes. For we believe God has acted. He has shown His power. His purposes for this nation."

"Isaiah, eat that pie and cease your preaching, please. My gloom is, as you say, inappropriate to the celebration. Forgive me. It is just that I am troubled by what we have established. I want peace, in which I can prosper. That had best been promoted by the King coming to some accommodation with his victorious Parliament. I accept that. It did not happen so, because he proved faithless and a liar. We are where we are. Now come, let me fill your glass and let us have another toast. Come Susanna, father, I give you… friendship." And he held up his glass, looked Isaiah in the eyes, and said, "To friendship. Born of endurance and shared experience in troubling times."

*

Noah had been at Worcester fight.

It was as well that Musgrave's had left Bristol with several wagons containing barrels of biscuit. Nathaniel Musgrave knew the effect of famine upon men's spirits. The King, who had expected thousands to join him, saw none. But the English went, in their thousands, into the ranks of their county militias, to fight against his Scots. And the challenge for the Parliamentary leaders was to feed such a great host. So Nathaniel Musgrave's foresight was providential.

Scots arms were seen by the English as coming to impose the Presbyterian religious system south of the border. England's angry response was to put thirty-one thousand soldiers under the command of Oliver Cromwell, who concentrated them at Worcester. By his tactical mastery, using pontoon bridges to move his men, Cromwell beat the royal army and scattered it. Once again the demoralised Scots were led by their incompetent nobility to ruin. And, this time, even further from their homes.

Noah was in the second rank, immediately behind Hezekiah, when Musgrave's stood to the east of Worcester City. Confident in his numbers, Oliver had divided his force — and the main battle raged well to the south and west of the city where the River Severn was joined by the gentler waters of the Teem. Noah could hear the concussion of guns, the cacophony of musketry and hatred. Musgrave's stood in silence looking at the city, and wondering — hoping — that the whole affair would be completed without their participation. It did not occur to any of them that this fight might be lost. The mood was optimistic. In their ranks they kept quiet — "Silence!" having been Sergeant Hollin's last order — but there were squadrons of horse drawn up on the Regiment's right, and Noah could see the troopers smoking their pipes. Their laughter and chat sounded shrill and noisy, irreverent above the silence of the infantry.

Colonel Musgrave himself sat his horse at their front. It was a fine black mare and their Colonel had on his red-feathered hat. He was observing the city through a perspective glass. The road out of Worcester towards London passed through their position, well to Noah's left, Musgrave's being on the extreme right of their position.

They all knew that the Scots King intended to move on his capital. Noah and his comrades were firm that, if he did so, he would meet his ruin. For he would have to get past them. Musgrave's. The best. This confidence was not spoken of, not debated. It was a fact, lying deep in the psyche of each man there.

For the greater part of the day, they stood silently in their ranks and files blocking the road from Worcester. They were on higher ground, on a heath looking down at the city. They could see its fortified outline, the lovely river flowing behind it from the right to their left, and the great cathedral with its tower. Where the road entered the city they could see a great earthwork of fortification thrown up by the royal army.

Rebecca was suddenly beside him. She thrust at him a hunk of bread and a lump of cheese. She placed a flask of water between his feet, laid her fingers upon his lips, looked into his eyes, passed food to Hezekiah too, then moved behind them, and was gone. Hezekiah winked at Noah and they ate. Noah drank from the flask and passed it to Hezekiah, and back to others. Rebecca had a gift for finding food.

Sergeant Hollin moved amongst them, giving permission for files to fall out for brief relief. When their turn came, and they were in the rear, pissing, Hezekiah said to him, "I like this fucking idleness, Noah." He gave a great fart. "That's all I'm doing today. The Scots will go home now." They laughed. Back in the ranks, the silence resumed.

To their front, Nathaniel Musgrave still sat without moving. Noah was watching him, and saw him take off his hat and mop his brow. It was a fine August day, but there was a light wind cooling them. Noah saw his Colonel suddenly stand up in his stirrups, waving to others and then pointing down towards the city. There was a vibration in the ground as a series of officers rode up to assemble around Nathaniel Musgrave. A conference was taking place. For the moment all Noah could see was the back end of several horses.

Hezekiah looked at Noah over his shoulder, and pulled a grimace.

The assembly of officers dispersed, and Noah's interrupted view forward was restored. And he could see what had excited his commander. From the city, a column of troops was emerging, grey-clad figures, deploying across the road. After a few minutes they had formed into two lines, and paused to dress their ranks, gathering themselves. Then they began to advance and to Noah, awaiting them, drum beats were an audible mark of their menace. Then Musgrave's own drums thumped out, drowning their opponents' more distant noise. Nathaniel Musgrave had dismounted, sending his horse to the rear and grasping in his hand his spontoon. They checked their dressings and waited.

In his position as the extreme right wing of Oliver's army, Colonel Nathaniel Musgrave was in close liaison with the flank guard of horsed troopers, who in the next two hours hovered close by his Regiment's right, ready to forestall any move by Scots horsemen to outflank them.

No such threat materialised. Fighting was continuing to the south and west and this had absorbed the best and the majority of the royal army. The force that came against them was the reserve that had been holding

Worcester, now thrown away in what never was their sides' main effort. Nonetheless, they came on manfully.

It was clear that the Scots attack was centred upon the road and therefore to their left. They watched the grey clothed infantry of their enemy stoutly walk forward into the destroying musketry of the red coats to their left. The affair disappeared in the smoke of exploding powder. With one eye upon Worcester city, Colonel Musgrave drew his regiment's right side files forward, faced them to slant towards the Scots flank, and proceeded to deliver fire by ranks into the side of the mass of grey men. When his turn came, Noah delivered his shot, peeling off as he was trained to do, to take his place at the rear, loading his piece as he went. The Scots were so tightly packed, the angle at which the fire was delivered was such that the slaughter of the invaders was remorseless and total. Within twenty minutes, what remained of them was in flight back the way they had come.

Musgrave's drums had his regiment in order immediately, their front realigned. Leaving their match, file by file they went again to their rear to restock their powder and ball. Then, back in their ranks and files, as the regiments to their left began to move forward, towards the town, Noah and his comrades too began a measured, remorseless advance.

There was no resistance until they were within musket shot of the fort that Noah had observed earlier.

Musgrave's were advancing steadily, and in front of them they could see the earth dyke that was the wall of Worcester. There was a ditch in its front, and the fort was to their left, where Musgrave's flank would come close. Then the defences erupted fire. There was a deafening noise. All was enveloped in a mass of acrid smoke, and the buzz of death-dealing lead was zipping into their ranks. Their drums quickened their pace, then had them at the double. Noah heard Sergeant Hollin yell, "Club y'r musk...," then formation was lost as Musgrave's ran forward into the ditch, up the earth bank and into Worcester. Noah went with them.

He was over the top of the rampart and Hezekiah was there too. He could see men running, presenting their retreating backs to the incoming victors. He was close behind Hezekiah, when his friend stopped moving, momentarily stood still, then fell back into Noah. His musket dropped against Noah's shins, and Noah caught him, seeing that his mouth was open, and that there was only blood and darkness where his forehead had been. Noah immediately thought, *Oh bugger!*.

He let his friend fall to the ground.

The beating of the drums for Musgrave's to recover their order, asserted his training and he took his place in his rank, then shuffled forward to lead, taking Hezekiah's place. He was shaking. Sergeant Hollin moved across his front, dressing the line with his halberd. If he saw that Hezekiah was gone, he said nothing. On the open ground immediately within the ramparts of Worcester, the regiment fell again into its order. Nathaniel Musgrave halted his advance and held his men there.

The fighting was dying away. The royal army was beaten out of its position and was either in flight or begging for quarter. To their left rear, the fort had fallen into silence.

Worcester itself ahead of them was shrouded in smoke, there was fire visible in several places and a babble of noise. What streets they could see were crowded with grey-clad figures hurrying away; in disorder, Noah could see. There were no lines of men, only their hurrying, jostling backs as they sought to put distance between themselves and their defeat.

Captain Parker spoke to Sergeant Hollin who turned to Noah's division. "Stand easy," shouted the sergeant. This released them to talk but Hezekiah was not there to talk to. Noah felt his legs shaking, and looked at his feet. Both hands gripped his musket, his head fell forward and he wept.

*

Stung by complaints that royalist fugitives were going abroad from Lynn — *his* Lynn — its Parliamentary governor, Colonel Valentine Walton, had deployed his best efforts into frustrating such escapes. He had placed himself effectively across this route out, and was choking it off. It was not known to Simon, but Master Humbold would in future receive more cash from turning in a fleeing royalist than he would ever be paid for sailing him in *Ariel's Kiss* across the North Sea.

George Chennery made the mistake of thinking that, since he had escaped England once before through Lynn, he could do it again. Departing after the disaster at Worcester, he came to the town in the disguise of a merchant. George was ever an alert observer of his surroundings, and despite his injuries at that time, he knew from his earlier visit how to find Simon. He had decided the route had served well in the past and would do so again. Matters were quickly arranged.

Sadly, someone else also knew all about Simon's clandestine activities — or at least, knew enough. The new reality in Lynn was being created by Parliament's money, and so while George was not without means, and paid Simon well, it was Isaiah Yates that slipped all the shipmasters of Lynn their larger bribes. He had sums to disburse that would seal up King's Lynn against any royalist traveller. All were on the lookout for Charles Stuart himself, but the smaller fry were not escaping the net.

At precisely the correct moment, Isaiah appeared upon the quayside with a half-dozen musketeers. He had watched George Chennery go aboard Humbold's ship. He noticed how unsteady the fugitive was and correctly concluded that the last few weeks had fatally damaged George's health, his body not having ever recovered from its earlier injuries.

Given that its master was now suborned, the matter went swiftly forward and silently the crew of *Ariel's Kiss* pointed Isaiah's squad correctly towards the cabin.

Isaiah's party was armed with pistols, the army recognising that policing a port, requiring as it did frequent clambering on boats and inside ships, was best done with a handy weapon rather than a cumbersome musket. Isaiah had his own long horse pistols. He had thought, from his glimpse of George Chennery, that it was most unlikely he would need either, since the man looked too weak to fight.

Isaiah felt that matters were proceeding well. He silently descended the companionway that led to the master's cabin, leading his group. He had reckoned without Simon. Observing all that was happening, and angry at the betrayal of his plans by Humbold, the young man ran up onto the ship, came behind the soldiers and launched himself at the rearmost, sending them all, by his impetus, falling down into an undignified heap outside the cabin door.

Isaiah's companions picked themselves up and began to contain Simon, who was fighting them all, fierce fists jabbing at them and feet landing kicks. It was a few seconds before a pistol shot ended his intervention, the force of the ball throwing Simon's body across the narrow and gloomy space. He fell to one side, his limbs sprawling and his life ebbing out of him in a great flood of blood.

Isaiah understood immediately that any chance of taking George Chennery prisoner by surprise was now gone. But he quickly perceived that since the man was so obviously ill, there would be no resistance. He flung open the door, and found himself looking into the small cabin that was the master's accommodation.

Isaiah saw through the stern windows of *Ariel's Kiss* the port of King's Lynn going about its usual business. He saw also that sitting behind a small table in the midst of the cabin was his quarry. He took in, too, that George Chennery was himself holding a pistol. But it was not pointing at Isaiah, it was pointing up into George's own mouth.

Isaiah, ever the soldier, both dived to one side and levelled his own gun. There was a crashing bang as two pistols went off in the confined space. George fired, sending his own brains across the room to splatter upon the window behind him. His body jerked backwards, his head falling to hang down behind, and his shattered skull emitted a cascade of red blood.

Isaiah stood for a moment, and deep despair put a cold hand upon his heart. One of his men was now close behind, the smell of the man's breath clear to him in that small room. Isaiah turned to see the others craning their necks to look.

"He's dead," Isaiah said to them, harshly.

He went outside and looked down at Simon's body. One of his companions said, "He's dead too, sir." Isaiah gave him a withering look.

Then he said, "Stanton, get the master," and seeing Humbold approaching down the companionway, he said to him, "Right, mister, this is what you do. You go to sea as you planned. You get out there, and you bury these two out in the ocean. Understand? Do whatever it is you do — stitch 'em up with a cannon ball, eh? You do that. You get back here, and you tell Colonel Walton you have done as I say. And I will see that you get paid something extra for your trouble."

The master nodded, he was not about to let any issues interrupt a swift ending to this business. He said, "They died at sea, then."

Isaiah did not turn to look again at the corpse in the cabin, but went up the stair to the deck. He needed fresh air. He stood for a moment, looking at the port going about its business. Sea gulls were giving voice. He felt immensely weary. He recalled Josiah's greeting at their last meeting, and said out loud, but to himself, "It is time you went home and stayed there."

About the Author

Oliver Woodman is a retired 70 year old living in Lichfield. In a former life he was a local government Personnel Officer. In even earlier times he studied for a career in the church. He has a wife, two adult offspring, and four grandsons, all of whom know of his love and knowledge of history.

Printed in Great Britain
by Amazon

10517764R00079